TALES OF THE FORGOTTEN GOD
BY DAN HAMILTON

THE BEGGAR KING
THE CHAMELEON LADY
THE EVERLASTING CHILD

TALES OF THE FORGOTTEN GOD

THE

EVERLASTING CHILD

Dan Hamilton

Illustrated by
Jack Stockman

INTERVARSITY PRESS
DOWNERS GROVE, ILLINOIS 60515

© 1994 by Dan Hamilton

Illustrations © 1994 by Jack Stockman

All rights reserved. No part of this book may be reproduced in any form without written permission from InterVarsity Press, P.O. Box 1400, Downers Grove, Illinois 60515.

InterVarsity Press® is the book-publishing division of InterVarsity Christian Fellowship®, a student movement active on campus at hundreds of universities, colleges and schools of nursing in the United States of America, and a member movement of the International Fellowship of Evangelical Students. For information about local and regional activities, write Public Relations Dept., InterVarsity Christian Fellowship, 6400 Schroeder Rd., P.O. Box 7895, Madison, WI 53707-7895.

Cover art: Jack Stockman

ISBN 0-8308-1673-9

Printed in the United States of America ∞

Library of Congress Cataloging-in-Publication Data

17	16	15	14	13	12	11	10	9	8	7	6	5	4	3	2	1
08	07	06	05	04	03	02	01	00	99	98	97	96	95	94		

For Andrew Stuart Hamilton—
prototype Child, Threeblade the Fierce,
ready companion, and bearer of my image

—CONTENTS—

Character Names

Old	New
Abra	Trueteller
Candolel	Candle
Kali	Moonflower
Roadreeler	Roadreeler
donkey	Kingsburro
Damon	Lionheart
Damon's niece	Woodswaif
Barid	Wordsmith
hunchback	Woebearer
Beauty	Beauty
the ancient enemy	Fame, Twister, Fortune, Mesmer, Mummer
Ellard	Binder
two orphan boys	Firecolt and Flamerider
Chameleon Lady	Brightface
Seareaper	Deedtester
Wavewatcher	Joykeeper
Foamrider	Seaswallower
Fearshadow	Dreadnought Freeblade
Andin	Stonesetter
Carlin	Featherstone
Sabrin	Sabrin
eagle	Farsight Featherfriend
Grimshade	Westerkeep
Heartbreak (village)	Heartshope
Darmak	Skymarker
Arden	Halfhand

—PREFACE—

Once there was a City where dwelt the Elder God and the men and women and animals and wonders he had made. All shone, all had joy, and all were loved.

But there were ways to leave the City—paths that were still forbidden to the people though left open to their feet, avenues made not by the Elder God, but by his old enemy who hated good things everywhere. All that the people needed was given them freely, but they were not content as long as the untrodden paths to the unexplored wilderness shimmered in the sun. So they left one day, first by ones, and then by groups, until they had all left the City to see what lay beyond. The Elder God called after them all, but curiosity deafened them and stopped their ears.

First the wilderness lay before them, then beside them on either hand,

and then it surrounded them. The wilderness terrified them, for there were lions there, and wolves, and fierce things that lived in the sea. Darkness fell upon them, and rain and thunder—the sad voice and tears of the Elder God. The world was changed in a great shaking and windstorm; the people turned, but could not find the way back to the City. Too late they understood that the roads would have been theirs to explore, and the wonders beyond theirs to conquer, had they waited until they had been tested, approved and empowered. Instead, they went in their own strength, and it was the wilderness which conquered them.

The City was never lost; it was only removed from the face of the earth and still was—somewhere. But the people were lost, and it was the path back to the City that was forfeit.

The people made themselves a king, to remind them of the Elder God, but no man falsely exalted could truly fill the empty throne. The people built Glory where they believed the City had been, but it was only a wicked and flimsy shadow. Some thought there might still be a secret door, and behind it a dark and dangerous path to the City, winding its way back if only one could plumb its mysteries. But if there was a door leading to such a path, it was hidden, and no one knew where it was. Each year fewer searched for the fabled door, and then the people lost count of the years. Glory endured, and they still crowned kings, but the memory of the Elder God largely faded from the land. In few places was he still worshiped; in no place was he altogether without a witness.

Then the beggar came. Covenant. The beggar who reigned as a quiet king. The dusty man who spoke for the Elder God and changed lives around him frequently and forever. The one who bent the twisted world around him so that those who stood with him could see its true shape. The man who raised the dead to life again and granted rest to the bone-weary. The traveler who defeated fire and fired the defeated to new heights of courage and honor. The patient man who sifted the refuse of the world and recovered men and women and children (and even the animals) and made them whole again in the midst of their imperfections.

Those he redeemed he called to his house in Glory. The old stone ruin was weathered and unremarkable from the outside, but on the inside it was a wonderful warren of comfortable rooms and kitchens and places to meet and eat and heal. And behind one particular door lay the path to the City.

This part of the story was told in *The Beggar King*, and the record was continued in *The Chameleon Lady*.

Covenant called more to his side, changing them even as he beckoned, with unexpected love and surprising authority.

A man who had long sought a hero's face discovered his answer both in Covenant and in kneeling before him. A woman with too many faces found acceptance and her true image through the beggar's hand and guidance.

Covenant's house resounded with words of welcome for the weary and wounded, fresh food for the famished and friendless, and scarcely returnable love for all.

Far beyond the walls of Glory, Covenant had left few corners of the kingdom untouched. By the sea, he had returned to life a boy who could not live in the water and fish that could not live out of it. Upon the sea itself he had delivered a hermit from the vicious shadows of his own past. In the mountains he had given new hope to a family who could not protect themselves from wolves. And Covenant's ransomed wine had brought release to a village of lepers.

The Company of Covenant grew and prospered—until the king fell ill and died. In the tumult of the tournament that followed, the unthinkable happened: Covenant challenged his old enemy Fame—and died. A mammoth stone crushed Covenant into the ground, though none could find any trace of his body save the spreading blood.

The Company had fled Glory even as the new king's men were coming for them, under orders to pull down the House of Covenant. Now they huddled in a village abandoned even by the lepers, a place made safe for them by isolation and contempt.

And now what? Covenant had called them, but where was he? Their hope was dead, their enemy sat unchallenged upon the throne of Glory, and they themselves were hunted men and women.

── ONE ──

Dreams
and
Darkness

FREEBLADE PACED THE DARKNESS IN HEARTSHOPE, HIS HEART
heavy even as he kept lone watch over the Company.

If I had only fought Fame myself, he whispered to himself in his
misery, *I might be dead, but Covenant would still be alive. How can I
undo my failure? I could not rise to fight with my weapon, and he fought
in my place without one—and in the end it was no weapon that slew him.*
His body still ached from his wounds and fever, but his mind
tortured him worst of all. *I should walk off into the forest and fall
on my sword. But then I would have failed my commission not once but
twice, and died a coward's death as well.*

In the houses, each member of the band of refugees was
also troubled, seeking the deeper sleep in vain. Their dreams
swirled around Covenant the beggar—starting with the moments when he had invaded their lives and left them forever

changed, and ending with those final moments that would fade from no one's mind. There was no hope of forgetting the sickening fear that became dull, monstrous certainty once they had rolled away the stone that had been toppled down upon the beggar. The blood that had stained the sand had marked their memories as well.

Even the restless sleep failed the Company at last. Though there were no lights in the sky yet but the stars, most shook off the tattered dreams and drifted outside, joining Freeblade where the night fire slumbered orangely in its pit. Numb and worn, none of them were surprised to find the others there; they assembled together in their unspoken need to be anything but *alone*. Rousing the fire again, they huddled wordlessly before the flames, seeking a warmth that was not there.

Full shock had set in now, and where they had been able to function and plan and act in the hours after Covenant's death, now they had no strength or emotion in reserve and could only stare with unseeing eyes at the devouring fire. Each one drifted, trapped in relentlessly circling thoughts.

Wordsmith weighed the sum of the dead Covenant's words to him. Wordsmith's wife, Beauty, wondered whether it had been the beggar's promises or the beggar himself that had failed.

Binder and Brightface clung tightly to one another's hand, their bodies not yet accustomed to the committed presence of the other. Their marriage—only two days old—had begun bravely on the edge of the horror, but could not avoid the plunge into sorrow. And Brightface was still shaking herself free from the internal shadows of her life as the Chameleon Lady.

Lionheart sat on the edge of the circle, thinking not only of Covenant but of the weight of orphans and elderly left in his care.

The first hint of dawn came at last upon them, following slowly along the wake of the long and wretched night. Defying the exhaustion and depression of the Company, the blooming light bore promise of a world continuing unchanged about them.

Wordsmith gazed up at the edge of the young sun in a sky still flecked with stars. "Our first hope is gone," said Wordsmith, "but the stars have been shining all night—and the sun has not failed us either." As they heard his thoughts, their words and wan smiles began to bubble to the surface again.

"Wordsmith," asked Brightface, her tears surprising her again, "who *was* Covenant?"

"*Was* he the Elder God?" added Binder.

"I thought so," answered Wordsmith, "and so I still believe. I cannot accept his death, yet I cannot explain it either."

The others stirred, as though waiting for the right words to spark them from their despair.

"All over this land," he continued, "there must be prayers rising to the Elder God. The invisible, the silent, the patient— he *must* be patient if he holds all power, yet is content to be nearly invisible and silent. If this world continues without Covenant here to see it, then perhaps we should continue as well."

Freeblade roused from his own stupor and declared, "Your words have shamed me, Wordsmith. Fame will be looking for us, and it is not fit that your champion should lie in the grass and wait to be taken. We do not even know what is to hand here—we know not where to hide, what to defend or how best to retreat. I must go and explore." He strapped on his sword, which had never been far from his hand.

"I will go with you," said Lionheart. "I cannot bear to do nothing. I do not regret the decision that brought us here, but how will my children and elderly survive? We are far from any help here—what food we brought with us will soon be gone, and I do not know where more will come from. Planting seeds will not suffice, for tomorrow's harvest cannot feed yesterday's hunger."

"There was always food and enough through Covenant," offered Beauty. "He sent me out into the streets many times to gather food from kind and generous strangers."

"But now we have no Covenant—and no streets either, and no strangers to fill them," replied Lionheart.

"The lepers had food to eat, didn't they?" countered Beauty. "They were dying slowly every day, but they were not starving. There must be food nearby."

"Let us look," said Wordsmith simply. The three of them walked away from the fire without further discussion.

* * *

After an hour they returned; Wordsmith and Beauty sat, with faint smiles on their faces, while Freeblade leaned against a rock, still looking dissatisfied and uneasy. Others joined them to hear their news.

"Though Covenant is not here," said Wordsmith, "we have not been forsaken."

"We are well provided for," explained Beauty. "The gardens of the lepers are just over this hill—all kept well-tended until the day they left. The ground bursts with vegetables, and the orchard groans beneath the weight of the fruit. Every good thing that grows is there, and a few recent weeds as well. All we need are pruning hands and strong backs to bear the baskets."

The rest heard and were comforted. The pall of desolation lifted a bit higher.

"There is water in abundance," continued Beauty, "both in the wells and in a stream that separates the gardens from the orchards. What else can we need? This place has been hidden in fear, disease and obscurity for many years—and now it is for us a haven."

Reluctantly, Freeblade spoke. "But I fear we cannot defend this place if we are attacked. There is no place to serve as a stronghold, no hills to hide behind, no trackless forest to lose ourselves in. We are simply *here*, and any who come after us may come upon us from any direction."

He shifted slightly, tension knotting his shoulders. "Nor can we mount a useful watch. Even a mightier company than this would not be able to disperse and watch all the wandering paths and meadows that one could follow to this place. Were it not for the food and for these houses standing ready for us, I would not stay here."

"But how can we travel any farther and stay together?" asked Brightface. "We have nothing left but our own feet."

Freeblade turned to Brightface, a wry smile on his face. "It is not a place I would choose to defend," he acknowledged. "But the Company is here, and I must defend it, for I will not bear this sword in vain."

Wordsmith spoke again. "We must be cautious, but not afraid. Let all our fires by day be small and smokeless, and let our fires at night be smaller and burn behind a cover of stone. Freeblade believes that the noise of the children playing will not carry as far as the main road to Glory, but in any case let us take the children each day to the meadows beyond the orchards."

"But will Fame even look for us here?" asked Binder. "Will he not think we have either hidden ourselves in Glory or fled to the ends of the kingdom?"

"I do not know," shrugged Freeblade. "We cannot hide here—or anywhere—forever, but let us shelter here while we may."

"If the lions answer me," said Lionheart, "there will be a guard on our borders tonight."

Wordsmith nodded, and began again. "We must eat again, for hunger is before us. We need not defend now, for our enemies have not found us."

"And let us do what work we can," suggested Beauty, "that we may be ready for whatever comes upon us next."

The sun crept higher, and the silence began to be broken by the calls of children and the querulous voices of the aged. The desire for meaningful work slowly came to them again, and they began to consider their practical needs and the harvest the lepers had left behind.

* * *

There was a second night, with its share of deep doubts and deeper loneliness, and a second morning with its promise of renewed hope.

The Company began to carve and claim a new routine, welcoming anything that laid a straight line and a goal for them; any task that was different and safe and productive would lighten their hearts and hasten their healing.

The children were somber for a while, reflecting the mood of their elders, but they quickly forgot their grieving and began to play.

"Children cannot grieve all at once, as we do," observed Brightface. "They will cry, and then laugh, and later cry again. Let them sorrow in their own way and time."

Still the Company drifted rudderless in the safety of their refuge. They talked little, thought much and cried often—either separately or together.

* * *

Binder saw Brightface kneeling before a quiet pool in the stream, and walked unheard to join her. He was startled to find her gazing into the water while a multitude of images flowed across her face. She sensed his presence, and even as she turned to him her true face was restored to its proper place.

"What . . . ?" gasped Binder, baffled and fearful and too weary to comprehend. "I thought you were healed! Or did the cure end with his death?"

"Nor did I know if his magic would linger," she said, "for I have already sought my reflection a hundred times in fear. Covenant did more than I could have guessed, for now I have the power to change my appearance. I *control* it; it no longer controls me." For an instant, she became a shriveled old woman, and then a beaming girl, and then herself again.

"Aren't you afraid to lose your face again?"

"No. It's not the same at all. I can feel the difference. I have to will a new face to carry it, and when I stop pretending it goes away. What was weakness is now strength." She rose and came to him, leaning against his chest and gazing up into his eyes. "But I won't do it again if it disturbs you."

"It disturbs me greatly," he admitted, "though I suppose it could be useful someday."

* * *

By sundown all were tired, all were dirty and all were full. Most surrendered willingly to sleep, with some measure of ease for the first time in Heartshope.

TWO

Words from the Wilderness

WORDSMITH WAS ALREADY READING HIS LITTLE BOOK OF Covenant's wisdom when the rest awoke.

"Are our answers there?" asked Freeblade.

Wordsmith shook his head slowly. "I may indeed have all the answers we need," he said, running his fingers along the edge of the tiny leather book of mysteries, "but if I do, I do not know it. They were not clear when I set them down and have been dark ever since. Yet they are less dense this morning, as though a mist is rising from my mind."

"What do you see?"

Wordsmith shook his head, frowning. "Things too vague for words—for now, anyway. I need more time."

"Time, at least, we have," observed Freeblade.

"Read, then," urged Binder. "We have our work to do, and

you have yours." Wordsmith nodded absently, already lost again in the puzzles of Covenant's words.

Through the following days and deep into the nights, he perused the pages as the Company rebuilt its life again. His heart grew weary with burdens, and his head ached with the pressure of thoughts he could not for long hold to himself.

The thoughts of the others multiplied too, and it was not unexpected that a council formed of its own accord before many days had passed.

Gathered about the fire one evening, the Company poured out its flood of questions before Wordsmith. He heard them all before asking quietly, "Why do you look to me for answers? I am not Covenant, nor do I claim to have his voice that I may speak to you."

"We must follow someone," answered Binder. "We are lost without a leader, and your words have been good for us."

"If you look to me for anything but words, you are lost even with a leader. Better you should at least follow a man with a sword."

"Nevertheless," said Freeblade, "I yield to you. No one else has spent so much time with Covenant."

"We can see that now," said Brightface. "He was preparing you to be our leader."

"I can only tell you what I have told you once already," insisted Wordsmith. "I will do what I must do, and you may follow if you see fit."

No one dissented, so Wordsmith was given the leadership he would not claim.

"Some burdens are hard," he said, "though some may be shared. I cannot do this alone. I must have help." He gazed at Beauty, and she could feel the heaviness of his heart, the resolution building to say what he knew he must say. "I would take Beauty and Freeblade to stand with me."

Beauty moved even nearer to him. Freeblade leaned against a nearby boulder where he could see the full circle of the fire and beyond. The shine of his sword in the flickering light held Wordsmith's eye for a long moment.

"Wordsmith," said Lionheart. "Talk to us."

"About what?"

"About the beggar. About Covenant."

Wordsmith nodded, but did not open his mouth immediately. They waited patiently for him to speak.

"When I chose to follow this beggar," he began slowly, still gazing at the sword or something far beyond it in the darkness, "or when he chose me to follow him, I began to find old and hidden promises coming true.

"Rumors of an Elder God. Prophecies of a man who would come in his name. Tales of a man who worked miracles and asked nothing in return, demanding no gifts and yet claiming loyalty.

"All those whispered shadows were cast by Covenant, and every deed confirmed his stature. And every word he spoke carried weight, whether it was clear or not.

"I could not deny the truth when I faced it at last. Nor could I debate its meaning, or avoid it. I could only see, and accept and bow. Even logic must kneel before the truth; and then the truth lifts up logic, and makes it whole again. So I bow before the truth, but my logic is not yet enlightened."

His voice grew more animated. "I think of all he said—words that were actually promises—and how those promises came to pass. The fulfilling of promises is power, and the fulfilling of great promises is great power.

"With his promises he blessed each of us, and to each of us he has given the desires of our heart, or pointed to a time when we would indeed receive them.

"Even the legend of the Judgment Stone proved true. Until it fell we had peace, of a sort. And now, I wonder if we shall pass into a time where there is no right or wrong—for who shall judge? And where will he sit?"

The question went nowhere, and he continued: "In Covenant I also found power, a kindly power that was greater than human energy and too compassionate to have come from the hand of humanity alone. His power has changed every one of you as well, or you would have no reason to be here.

"Promises and power. And he warned of a peril to come. We have all heard the promises, we have all felt the power, and now we have tasted the peril.

"But old promises, even ones that have been fulfilled, hold no power over the future. If our hope lies anywhere, it is in the words that he spoke to me in the wilderness, that I might write them down and preserve them, perhaps for this very moment.

"I must conclude that if these words are true—and they seem to be—and if he saw them from afar and named them rightly, then he must also have seen his death approaching. So his death must be either of such magnitude to destroy his promises or a thing of little moment, a stray but meaningless thing that cannot stand in his way.

"Now we must decide: Do we still believe his promises? Does the Elder God exist, and do we still put our trust in him?

"There is nothing that says we must. We could go our separate ways from here, and how could our enemies hunt us down in ones and twos? Surely Fame would not pursue us if we did nothing and were not to be found."

He paused, and tossed a fresh branch onto the fire.

"Yet in these promises are commands as well. And I cannot escape the weight of this one: 'When you seek me and do not find me, go and search for the Child upon the mountain.'

"There is truth we cannot escape: Covenant is dead—or at the very least, he is not *here*, and we may never see him again.

"I cannot delay any longer. I must go, even though I do not know what I will find or even how I will complete the task.

"Perhaps I should have gone immediately, even the day we arrived, but I did not. My hopes grew gray with sorrow, and I could no longer feel in my heart what my head knew to be true." Dejection shadowed his face.

"Do we have any other guidance, any counsel at all?" asked Brightface.

"We have only the words from Covenant," said Wordsmith. "We must wait for the meaning to be made plain."

Brightface sighed. "Words are such slight things to rest our hopes upon."

Wordsmith nodded. "Words are frail—a stroke of fading ink on parchment doomed to perish. But the promises are solid, even if the words used to mark them fade away."

"But how should we remember all of them?" asked Binder.

"Perhaps the time has come to engrave them all on our hearts. And perhaps in our minds joined we will find wisdom instead of worldly wonder, clarity against confusion, and light where all the light is lacking."

He read them the book aloud, shrinking not from the shrouded words and puzzling meanings that twisted back upon themselves. Every phrase was an echo of truth, every line bearing the ring of steel and striking fire from the stubborn flint of their hearts.

And for a time Covenant walked among them again, with his vague yet pointed words of death and birth, darkness and light, building and destruction, extreme sorrow and overwhelming joy. All tasted the goodness of Covenant's words, and none noted the passage of time. They listened, understanding little, but receiving much encouragement. *So many great things to happen,* they wondered. *Might they not happen soon?*

When Wordsmith finished, the spell took quite some time to fade.

"This book is an open secret," he eventually resumed. "But even he who wrote the words down cannot decipher them fully. Do not press me for explanations yet, for I still seek them myself."

"Not all of it makes sense," said Freeblade.

"It doesn't have to," replied Wordsmith. "As long as it's true."

"And we go to seek the Child?" asked Freeblade.

"I do."

"If you do, then we do. There need be no more discussion."

"We?"

"I hear. I believe," said Freeblade. "I will seek the Child, and serve him. I long to see this Child whom I am to defend."

"I, too, will go with you," said Beauty. "I vowed once to follow you, and confirmed my pledge a second time. I will not turn away from a third proof."

"It will be dangerous—with the danger of the completely unknown," Wordsmith cautioned her.

"I would rather suffer with you than be at ease without you. Besides, with your leg you will need help climbing."

"That is our challenge now," said Wordsmith firmly. "Find the Child, follow him, and protect him."

"Will we recognize him?" asked Freeblade.

"If he comes from Covenant we will surely know him," said Wordsmith.

"It is not always that easy," Freeblade responded. "I looked long to find the Dreadnought promised in the pages of my own ancient book, yet I knew him not when I met him."

"But how many children dwell upon the mountain?" asked Beauty. "There cannot be many, that we should have to separate one from the other."

No one could answer her question.

Their eyes turned to Lonely Mountain, lost in the invisible distance far over the trees and beyond Glory. "No one has climbed there successfully—and returned," said Beauty. "How can we go where no one has ever been?"

"We are under orders," said Freeblade. "That is all we need to know."

"We should be safe from Fame," Beauty said. "If this is the first place he will never look for us, then the mountain is the second."

"We must be prepared for bitter cold and privation," said Freeblade.

"And to bring someone back," added Beauty. "We fled with little good clothing, but we can borrow from one another."

"Is that our course?" asked Freeblade. "Will that be enough?"

"There is one other thing that burdens me," answered Wordsmith. "We must know if Candle and Moonflower have come to harm. And what has become of the House and its treasures."

"You mean go back to Glory?" Binder asked.

"I know of no other way to find out."

"But who will go?"

"I do not know who *can* go," responded Wordsmith, "let alone who *will*. Our faces are all known there."

"Not all of ours," said Brightface calmly.

"Yes, all of ours," answered Wordsmith sadly. "Be certain that Fame will not forget the faces of the men and women who cheered for Freeblade, or for Covenant."

"Watch this," countered Brightface. She blinked her eyes and shifted into the image of a total stranger. Complete silence fell, and she continued unhindered. "If Covenant's death has done nothing else, it has empowered me to bridle my burden and turn it to my bidding.

"But do not worry," she assured them, "it is temporary, and under my control." Her face snapped back into the newly familiar. "It is no longer a burden but a gift I may use for all. Let me return to Glory, without my chameleon cloak. I once walked through the palace unremarked, unrecognized and unchallenged. Surely I can reach the shop and even the House safely."

"I do not like that plan," stated Binder. "I cannot let you go alone, but how can I go with you and not endanger us all the more?"

Silence fell again until Freeblade's eyes chanced upon the

fire brothers, stalking each other through the edges of the forest. "We have two boys," he said, "who have proven themselves as courageous and resourceful as their elders. Perhaps they should go with Brightface."

Binder regarded them thoughtfully. "Firecolt. Flamerider. You have indeed proven your courage and your steadfast stealth in the open fields as well.

"Will you dare to go back to Glory with Brightface?" he asked. "A soldier carried you to the palace, but I think he cared more for the colors of your cloaks than the lines of your faces. And I have yet to meet the warrior who counted children among the enemies to be feared.

"For our sake will you become again nameless street urchins who do not know this lady openly, but can keep an eye on her? I cannot enter Glory safely, but I will hide in the woods within sight of the gate and wait for your return."

They looked at each other, thought for only a moment and said "Yes!" with one voice.

Binder looked at Lionheart, who nodded as well. "I do not know where the lions are," he said, "or I would send one with you. But I will go myself, and if trouble comes upon you I will return here for help."

Binder spoke to the boys again. "You *must* stay close to her— and if anything is wrong, come for me at once." He turned to Brightface. "Will you be content with those provisions?"

"Yes," she said. "Your love is your worry, and your worry is your love. I will go and not linger, and the boys shall watch over me."

"It is ironic," said Binder, "that Fame's hand should have fallen so heavily upon you, and yet you are the one with the best chance to watch him unseen."

"And the best motive, as well?" Her smile warmed the air between them before the discussion moved on.

"So we split into three parties," said Wordsmith. "Who will stay here?"

"I will," said Lionheart promptly. "My charges are here, and so are the animals."

"Then Heartshope is yours while we are gone, and I will not worry that care is lacking." He turned to Brightface and the fire twins. "We will accompany you as far as the last field before Glory, and from there you must journey on your own. We must reach the mountain with the first light of dawn, for we can neither face that climb nor climb that face in the dark, and we must return before the sun has set."

Binder shuddered. "I would not want to spend a night on that mountain. There is enough fear and madness in venturing there in the daylight."

"And if we do not find the Child?" asked Beauty.

"We will look the next day, and the next. There does not seem to be any choice but success."

Binder gazed at the three upon whom had fallen the responsibility of command—Wordsmith, Freeblade and Beauty. "He said in that book that Wisdom, Power and Love would rule us," said Binder. "I wonder if perhaps he meant you three."

Wordsmith avoided any reply by saying simply, "It is too late to leave tonight, and I would not travel during the day. Let us depart tomorrow, and leave tomorrow night."

The Company retired to their homes, seeking sleep to overcome their restless thoughts.

The next evening, while the others sought warm clothes and food for the road, Binder took time to rub dirt into the boys' clothes. "You have not been this crusty since my house burned," he muttered, "but you are too clean to pass for urchins."

At last, disguised for the city or carrying cloaks against the cold of the mountain, the travelers departed Heartshope in the heart of darkness.

* * *

The adventurers huddled together in the lee of the hill near Glory where the wilderness ended, hoping that the fading darkness had hidden them from the eyes of any searchers.

They paused, uncertain, four staring at the dawn-lit Glory, and the other three gazing ahead at Lonely Mountain.

Silently, but warmly, they parted.

Beauty and Brightface shivered, for different reasons.

─── THREE ───

The Hope
upon the
Mountain

CAUTIOUSLY, WORDSMITH AND BEAUTY FOLLOWED FREEBLADE through the deeply shadowed morning to the mountain. The gradually rising foothills did not begin to prepare them for its sudden stone reality; the sheer, cold cliffs leaped up immediately and unexpectedly from the landscape, towering high above everything around.

Even as they neared its base, cold vapors reached out and enveloped them in chill welcome. Still on the ground, their breath fogged their faces. Only a few feet above them frost tainted the bare rock, and above that ice and then only snow and mist.

"Is there a way up?" breathed Wordsmith, staring.

"There must be," answered Beauty, "if we are to climb it."

"We will be cold," said Freeblade. "Even these heavy cloaks

will not be enough." They looked at the pitifully thin clothes they had brought with them.

"Let us lay a fire here," suggested Freeblade. "We will be cold when we return." He gathered fallen wood into a pile and left tinder beneath it. The others took this last opportunity to eat something from their packs.

"What else do we need to do before . . . ?" asked Beauty, gesturing up at the unseen heights.

"Fill our water flasks again," Freeblade replied. "We have food enough for a day's expedition, but all the water up *there* is frozen."

They refreshed their flasks from a icy rivulet that trickled down the mountain and spread to nothingness in the grass.

They stood, silent, reluctant to begin the only task remaining.

"I brought several ropes," said Freeblade. "We must fasten ourselves together."

"A wise idea," said Wordsmith.

"Is that not more dangerous than each one alone?" asked Beauty.

"Perhaps, perhaps not," shrugged Freeblade. "One cannot slip without the others knowing, and having their weight to support."

"Besides," Wordsmith added, "if we perish, we perish together."

"Shall I lead the way?" Freeblade asked in jest.

Neither one prevented him.

"I will come last," said Beauty.

"No," stated Wordsmith flatly. "You will go in the middle. I want you where I can see you. I do not dispute your choice to be here," he continued warmly, "but I am concerned for you."

"And I am concerned for you," she responded. "Why can you not go ahead where I can see that you are safe?"

"As long as you feel a pull on this rope, I am there, and I am safe behind you."

They could think of no other preparations to make. Walking awkwardly against the unaccustomed strain of the ropes, and holding their worn robes tightly about them, they started up the mountain.

Within the first few minutes, Freeblade lost hope of any trail. For the moment, *forward* and *backward* were devoid of meaning; here there was only *up* or *down*.

* * *

Immediately they were glad of both the robes and the ropes. The uncommon chill began to gnaw their skin through every gap, and Freeblade did not wish to imagine how quickly they would be numbed without their cloaks. Then Beauty slid twice her own height when a rock crumbled beneath her feet; even as the men pulled her back to safety, the vision of another crumbling stone played in her mind.

Nor was she alone indebted for long. Freeblade promptly disappeared in a flurry of white crystal, breaking through a dome of frozen snow. Wordsmith anchored Beauty, and she led the warrior back to where they supposed the path to be.

Mist and fog pressed in between them as they ascended, leaving their figures blurred and uncertain and their voices thin and wandering. What had begun as mere frost was fast becoming ice. Every step was a hazard, every grasp a hope, every breath a prayer.

The sun, growing higher but no stronger, hid itself in the mist. The unseen ground receded beneath them. Their lungs ached from frost and fear and effort.

The hours passed painfully and relentlessly.

Freeblade stopped abruptly and beckoned them upward to see old bones—a withered skeleton entombed in the ice. A few moments later they discovered another nameless body.

"Did wild animals kill them?" Freeblade wondered aloud. "Hunger? This undying cold?"

"Not wild animals," Beauty said thinly against the biting wind.

"Why not?" grunted Freeblade.

"Have you seen any?" she asked in turn. "Have you seen *any* signs of life?"

"You're right," admitted Freeblade. "No trees, no plants, no birds—not even tracks of beasts in the snow. We are alone here."

"I hope not," replied Beauty. "The Child must be here if we are to find him."

They paused, almost dead themselves with cold and fatigue, wondering if their hopes held more life than their bodies.

"Is there nothing to this mountain but ice?" Wordsmith asked of no one in particular, exasperated.

But upward they pushed, putting more frozen wasteland behind and beneath them, while the pale sun passed over their heads and began to slide down before them.

"We are doomed if we do not turn back soon," panted Freeblade. "Night on this mountain will be worse than anything we have encountered yet. If we fail to move, we die."

And then Beauty saw the Child.

— FOUR —

Rubble
and
Ruin

FIRECOLT AND FLAMERIDER SLIPPED INTO GLORY AND QUICKLY disappeared into the winding streets.

"Who will you be?" whispered Binder to Brightface, watching them go. "It is fit that I know you when I see you again."

"Will this do?" She faded into someone he had seen in the streets ten thousand times—a nondescript woman, worn with weary years and almost featureless in her battered cloak.

"No one will look twice," she promised.

"No one but me," he added.

When her turn came, she paused only briefly at the gate, raised her hand a few inches in farewell and left Binder hidden in the shadow of the trees.

* * *

Candle looked up when Brightface entered his shop. He

moved toward her, unable to see clearly through the piles of bright cloth and the displays of fine items brought from the corners of the kingdom.

"Do not say my name aloud," she cautioned him in a whisper.

"How can I, my woman?" he asked in surprise. "I do not know what it is."

Brightface let her temporary face ease away to reveal her own.

Candle only nodded, though his eyes grew wider. "You are alone?" he asked as he moved behind her to draw the blind.

"Not quite," she murmured. She resumed her common face and leaned outside to smile at the urchin playing near the door.

Candle looked, just in time to see two boys swept away in a swirl of dirty children. Candle closed the door and bolted it firmly from the inside.

"Upstairs," he said, "but let me go first. Neither Trueteller nor Moonflower needs surprises—even pleasant ones."

Moonflower was asleep, but Trueteller hugged Brightface fiercely. "Is everyone all right?" she asked Candle over Trueteller's shoulder.

"I don't know," he answered. "I haven't asked her. She just got here."

Trueteller stepped back and eyed Brightface. "All alone?" she asked, astounded.

"No," soothed Brightface. "The boys are watching in the streets, and Binder is waiting beyond the gate."

Then the women both began to ask questions at once, until Candle held up his hands. "Peace!" he said warmly. "Let Brightface ask, and let us answer her questions. When Moonflower wakes, we will turn the questions around."

Brightface took a breath and began. "I came to see if you were all right, and to find out what has happened since we left."

"As you can see," said Trueteller, "we are well, and we have been left alone. As for what happened after you left . . ." She waved the attention to Candle.

"Glory has been in a quiet uproar," he explained. "No one knew quite what Fame would do. You saw how the first thing he formed was his army, picking captains and soldiers and filling the ranks with men like himself, or with men blinded by the power of his image and the promise of power themselves.

"With his men he came to seize us at Covenant's House, but we were gone already, thanks to Wordsmith's foresight and wisdom."

"What happened to the House?" Brightface probed.

Candle hesitated, sadness and anger rising together behind his eyes. "It has been pulled down—ravaged in anger and left in ruins. Every good thing there was carried off, and even the better stones have been dragged away."

"Was there *nothing* left?" she pressed.

"This was all of meaning that I could rescue from the House," he said, opening a fragrant wooden box and offering it to Brightface. She took the box and found only a few fragments of lightly colored glass—all carefully framed now with rich and intricate wood.

"These were all that were left from the mirrors," he said. "I took the liberty to make frames for them. I was afraid they would break apart otherwise."

She held them to the light, one by one, and gazed into them. "They reflect nothing," she said at last, "and I cannot see through them either."

"There may be no power left in them," Candle admitted, "but this fragment in the dark frame is from the mirror in the hall by the door to the City—at least, where the door was. It is completely blocked now, and would take an army an age to uncover again.

"The other pieces are from the rubble of the tower. This

bigger piece, I believe, is from one of the four windows, while this thick, wavy glass must be from the fifth."

"Thank you for rescuing them," she said quietly, holding them out to him. "Please keep them safe until . . . until something good happens again."

"They should be in your hands," insisted Candle, folding her fingers back over the fragile relics. "They may yet be of use again."

She gazed down at the remains, thinking about the simple dignity of the House. "Is this everything?" Brightface asked, disappointed. "It seems so little to remind us of so much."

"I also returned to the arena," Candle continued. "And I have bottled some of the sand soaked with his blood. It is all we have left of him."

"His words will stay in my heart longer than his blood in the sand," inserted Trueteller.

"Candle," asked Brightface abruptly, "is it safe to go to the House again?"

"Safe? I believe so. But is it a good thing?" She did not answer immediately. "You may certainly go to the House," he continued. "There is no one to stop you, and I do not know that anyone watches the House now that it has fallen. The devastation wrought by Fame is complete, and has left that place of little use to anyone but the mice and the crickets that make their nests in the stones. Stones lean and splinter and fall without warning, the floor is burned through in many places, and the few passages left standing are dark and still. I would not go to the ruins, if I were you. I have been there enough . . ." His voice trailed off expressively.

"Yet I will go and see," said Brightface.

"For yourself?" he asked.

"For all the rest who cannot see for themselves. They sent me to be their eyes and their ears and their witness in the town we had to leave behind."

He shrugged. "Let us wait until dusk, then. We will be less

obvious then."

"We? You do not have to go."

"I would feel better if I could watch over you. Surely Binder would want it that way."

"The boys report to him, and will see to my safety. Besides," she smiled, "they are invisible in the streets even when someone sees them."

"There is other news as well," said Trueteller darkly. "There was an earthquake the night Covenant died. It may even have helped Fame destroy the House."

"We felt the earth shudder," said Brightface. "Did Glory suffer as well?"

"Yes. Buildings fell, and people died. But death was not the worst thing to frighten the town. When they went to bury the bodies, the people found many old graves open and empty."

"So it was for us, too, at the graveyard of the lepers," said Brightface. "Empty graves and no bodies anywhere."

"Nothing has been said publicly," added Trueteller. "They buried the new bodies in the old places and went away quickly."

"Since then," said Candle, "we have hidden here, and trembled for our lives, and waited."

"Has anyone come for you?"

"No. Neither friend nor foe. You are the first to find us."

"Is Fame still searching?"

"Not heavily, for his men have other tasks on their hands. Heard you no word of it in the street?"

"No. I thought the people seemed subdued, but excited."

Candle nodded. "Exactly. Fame has captured their imaginations already, and has drawn them into a grand task together.

"He is building a tower. No small one, but an enormous monument to himself—where Covenant died, where the Stone of Judgment buried itself in the sand. The fallen rock is the cornerstone, and all the arena is marked to honor his grand design. It will be a strong fortress when he completes it. In less than a week it is further along than I could have imagined."

"Where is he finding all the stone?" Brightface wondered.

"From Covenant's House, in part, and from the palace, a place disdained by Fame as old and useless, a hollow ruin not worth rebuilding. Other stones have been carried in from the hills. No quake-tattered house or decaying inn is safe from the hands of his men. And the people are willing to help—giving of their strength, their time and their materials."

"I cannot say that I am surprised by this," said Brightface. "Covenant taught us that people and their names go together."

"Nor am I surprised, except to see that the people are behind him. A fever has gripped them all: 'Great is Glory,' they chant."

"If Covenant were still here this would not be happening."

Moonflower roused from her slumber then, and heard Brightface's voice but not her words.

"Candle?" she called. "Is someone here?"

They came to her, and she, too, was delighted to greet Brightface.

"You look tired, but happy," Brightface said, clasping Moonflower's hands.

Moonflower nodded. "I am already showing," she said, "but every day is still a trial, and food holds little interest."

"That will pass," said Trueteller.

They began to question Brightface then, and the hours passed as she told them of Heartshope and the decisions made there, of the spirit that had united them once again and of the quest upon the mountain for the promised Child.

"And now we wait," she concluded, "to see what will happen there, whether they prove the promise—or fail.

"But if they fail I cannot blame them," she added. "They have done the best they could."

Candle nodded. "Wordsmith should lead us," he said when

she was done speaking. "And Beauty and Freeblade to help him. You have chosen well."

The conversation passed to more general things, and she ate with them as they waited for dusk. After their meal, they savored their thoughts in silence, until Brightface rose to go.

Candle walked her to the shop door.

"There is other disturbing news," he said softly to her when they came downstairs. "Moonflower and Trueteller know of it, but find it a fearful thing to speak of: Moonflower may be the only woman in Glory with child.

"Even before Covenant died there were rumblings and rumors of barrenness throughout Glory, and Trueteller and I both still hear the fear and fact in the marketplace. For good or for bad, we had made no secret of Moonflower's condition, and all who live around us know. Indeed, the neighbor women seemed to know before we told them.

"There are already whispers, for no one seems to know of another woman with child who has not already been delivered."

"What does it mean?" Brightface asked anxiously.

"We do not know," he said, "but it disturbs us. These are not good times to come to public notice. Tell Wordsmith these things, and send us any counsel he has for us.

"Walk safely," he continued, "and give our care to the Company. We will wait here and be faithful."

Brightface looked out the door, and a small shadow detached itself from the deeper shadows to draw near to her. "I will," she whispered. "We go to see the House, and then to Binder and Heartshope again."

They waved to each other as the night separated them once more.

*　*　*

Brightface came first to the arena, where the foundations of Fame's tower surprised her by their size. A ring of boulders circled most of what had once been open sand. The fallen

Stone of Judgment had been tipped flat again as a cornerstone and mortared over with a new layer of stone. The new wall was not high enough to be seen over the other buildings, but if its final height matched its width it would someday be visible for miles.

Within the great circle was a smaller spire of rock, thrusting even more urgently to the sky. Although night was approaching, the work continued unabated; torches circled the arena and flickered in every corner, casting their uncertain light over the soldiers and townspeople moving earth and stone and lumber.

Brightface shuddered, and moved resolutely toward what was left of the House.

* * *

Brightface was crying silently when the boys accompanied her back to Binder.

"Covenant's death was bad enough," she told him, "but there was no body to see. Now I have seen the wreck of his House, and it grieves me more than I thought mere stones could."

They returned to Heartshope at once, bearing the light burden of gifts and the heavy burden of increased knowledge.

FIVE

The Child
of the
Snows

THE CHILD'S EYES WERE CLOSED, AND HE WAS HUDDLED IN A blanket of snow sitting upright against a dagger of ice. Beauty cried out and floundered through the frozen drift to his side. She snatched him up in her arms and wrapped his cold flesh into the warmer depths of her cloak. Beauty groaned in her throat, making sounds of hope against the cold and pain and fear.

"Is he alive?" Wordsmith shouted to her.

"I don't know," called Beauty miserably. "He's cold, so cold."

The two men reached her and gathered around to shield her from the unforgiving wind.

"Let us see him," murmured Freeblade.

She pulled back her cloak a bit, and they all beheld his still face with blue lips and white face, iced hair and frosted eyelashes.

When he saw the Child, Wordsmith fell silently to his knees and gazed at the still form. A series of strange expressions passed over his face; amazement, illumination, wonder, sadness, joy, relief and contentment.

He stood again. "I understand much now that I did not see before," he whispered. "Our quest is fulfilled, though not finished. Behold the Child—the *Everlasting* Child!"

"He is beautiful," Freeblade whispered.

"Beyond words," agreed Beauty.

"Is he breathing?" asked Wordsmith.

"I cannot tell in this cold," said Freeblade. "There is too much mist and smoke in the air, and our own breath is in the way."

"I felt him move, I think," whispered Beauty. "He *is* alive."

Barely, thought Wordsmith sadly. *The Child was here, and we came too late.*

"Come," said Freeblade. "We have done as we were bidden— to find the Child. And if we do not return now, our bones will lie with the others. There is no place for life upon this mountain."

They immediately turned to retrace their wandering steps.

"Look," said Beauty, pointing to a few faint footprints trapped in the rigid snow. "His tracks descend from the top," she said in awe. "How did he get up there?"

* * *

Going down was both harder and easier than going up. Their hearts were lighter, but their burden was heavier, and it was difficult not to move too fast for their safety. Beauty cradled the still, silent form, while Wordsmith and Freeblade scrambled on either side to keep them from falling.

"Whatever you do, don't let go of him," cautioned Freeblade. "We have the rope, and *we* will save *you*."

The two men lowered her down the steepest parts but could not prevent slips and thuds and bruises. Beauty ignored everything save the Child, clutching the pale body to her chest, peering anxiously every few moments to see if he had stirred.

If she falls, thought Wordsmith, *I'll have to carry them both. She'll die before she lets go of him.* "Has he moved yet?" he asked her again.

"No," she answered, "but at least he is no colder than he was."

I cannot feel my body anymore, thought Freeblade fuzzily. *Is that good or bad?* At least he was unaware of the raw flesh, and the blood oozing from the countless cracks in his skin.

With only the hope in their hearts to fuel their bodies and fire their feet, they crept anxiously toward the hidden ground below. The falling sun left them deep in shadow, granting light only faintly to the fog over their heads.

They were deep in afternoon shadow when the mists drifted apart enough to show the welcome hills below. They half-slid and half-jumped the last few feet down the mountain and stumbled their way to the relative warmth of the low hill still painted orange by the edge of the setting sun.

Panting hard and crying, Beauty snatched off her cloak and the Child's and pressed his bare body to hers. "This is no time to be modest," she called. "Quickly!" Wordsmith joined her, and the marbled flesh pressed against their own was an agony of ice.

Freeblade paused long enough to kindle the fire awaiting ready at their feet, hoping it would not be seen from Glory. Then he wrapped his bared arms and cloak around the others. "Is he warm yet?" he asked.

"I cannot tell, for I cannot feel either his flesh or mine," she moaned. "Oh, Wordsmith, did we come in time?"

"I should have come sooner," he said despondently, "but I delayed from day to day before yielding to the need. If we lose him now, it will be my fault."

"Or mine," she said, "for not having enough fire in my body to rekindle his. Wordsmith, how can you carry the blame for something you could not have foreseen—and that may not come to pass, anyway?"

He did not answer, except to say, "We did not plan well, did we?"

They coaxed the heat from the fire and urged it deep into the Child's bones, trying to ignore the pain of the spitting sparks and the singe of the flames licking about their legs.

"I cannot warm him enough," she mourned. "I would keep us both in the fire, if only our flesh would not burn."

"I was warmed once," Wordsmith said distantly, "far from any fire."

Beauty looked at him, memory of his tales bringing wild hope.

He released himself from their embrace, stalked to the edge of the firelight and faced the darkness squarely. Then he opened his arms to the fields and forests and called plaintively, "Animals of the Elder God, hear me. You warmed me once at Covenant's bidding. Come and warm another more worthy than I."

His words fell hollow in the night, and he dropped his hands to his sides again.

"Will they come?" whispered Beauty.

"Will who come?" asked Freeblade.

"The animals," answered Beauty absently.

A parade of eyes gleamed in the faint firelight.

"They could not have been far away," said Freeblade.

"Perhaps they were only waiting for your call," suggested Beauty to her husband.

"Do not be afraid, either of you," whispered Wordsmith. "I was, and all my worry was in vain."

Whimpering, the first lion thrust his muzzle between Beauty and Freeblade and licked the face of the Child.

"I was not sure I should try it again," Wordsmith said simply. "I feared that perhaps even one miracle was too much to hope for."

While Freeblade paced to watch and grow warm, Wordsmith

and Beauty moved to a softer place on the ground, beckoned the warm animals close and curled up in their midst with the Child. They watched the color of his face and listened for his breathing above the collected whuffs of the patient beasts.

"His hair is not frozen," Beauty said softly, "nor is that the firelight. It is the color of silver and snow, the color of gold and the sun. Never have I seen such a fair-haired child."

At long last the Child stirred, as if rousing from a deep sleep. Now his face looked more ruddy than pale, but it was hard to tell in the light of the fading fire. He did not open his eyes, but buried his face close against Beauty's breast.

For a moment, no one breathed but the Child.

* * *

Freeblade began to add more wood to the flames, then thought better of it; he left the fire to die away in its own time.

Above them in the darkness, the mountain began to moan and rumble, making long sliding sounds and venting prolonged hisses.

Wordsmith and Beauty scarcely heard, and paid little attention to what they did hear. Their exhaustion numbed them, and their world for now centered upon the sleeping boy held between them. But Freeblade's exhaustion left him tense and uneasy; he paced the rim of the firelight and listened with grave concern to the surrounding night.

"This mountain is too strange for us to bear it," Freeblade urged. "Let us be gone from here, even if we travel in the dark."

"Gladly," said Beauty, "if you will carry these animals or the fire in your hands, that we may slay the Child's chill, and our own."

Freeblade shook his head moodily and stared off into the night, trying so hard to hear everything that was there that he succeeded mainly in hearing those things that were not.

* * *

Wordsmith struggled awake in the dawn to find the animals

mostly gone. Only a pair of lions kept guard over the dead fire while Freeblade sprawled asleep on the ground.

Wordsmith roused Beauty with a touch of his hand and immediately, gently brushed the face of the sleeping Child, who opened his eyes and regarded them solemnly, without fear, without surprise.

"I have seen those eyes before," Beauty whispered. "He has come among us again!"

When the Child smiled, their hearts melted, and they forgot the snow and the ice and the remnants of the cold in their bones.

She spoke to him, asking his name. His smile grew wider and warmer, but he said nothing.

They roused Freeblade and rejoiced together in the new life that had come among them. As their eyes feasted on their hope, they feasted their hunger with the remainder of their food. The Child ate with an appetite, but contentedly—and silently.

"Wordsmith," whispered Beauty, "he is old enough to speak. Why has he not uttered a word?"

"Does he hear?" Wordsmith asked her. "Does he understand us?"

"He seems to understand my questions," she answered, "but all he does is smile and touch my hand. It is hard to be concerned about other things when I put his face close to mine."

"Perhaps he is a mystery to be understood later," Freeblade suggested.

But there was no clear answer to that question, and they continued with their silent meal. Wordsmith and Beauty had eyes only for the Child, but Freeblade's gaze also wandered frequently to the mountain. During the night the mist had multiplied, and the fog that hung far up the slopes had crept slowly and unnoticed down to the base. In several places water trickled down noisily and ran off into the grass—rivulets that had not been there before.

"The cold has gone," noticed Freeblade.

"Yes, we are all warm now," agreed Beauty.

"No, I mean the cold from the mountain."

He was right. Where dry, cold air had braced them before, now a river of moist air flowed down around them. It was no longer cold, but cool, and growing warmer by the moment. A greater mist was beginning to rise from the top—not wholly fog, but perhaps steam as well.

"Perhaps the mountain is melting," suggested Freeblade. "It seems to be more ice and snow than rock. Let us go. I do not understand this place, whether it means us harm or not, but something is happening here and I do not wish to see it from such a narrow distance."

"Is there any reason to linger?" asked Wordsmith.

"No," answered Beauty. "He is warm and well, and no longer hungry."

The Child walked about, unconcerned, seemingly unaware or forgetful of the ordeal on the mountain and the desperate race to pump warm life back into his thin body.

She knelt, took the Child's hand and spoke to him. "We must go from here. Will you go with us?"

The Child nodded and stood up.

The great lion also roused and came at once to crouch before the Child. The Child leaned up, grasped the great mane and pulled himself astride the shaggy back.

"I believe he is ready," said Beauty solemnly.

"Yes," agreed Wordsmith. "We are understood more than we understand."

* * *

Later, they paused and looked back at Lonely Mountain, small but still clearly visible in the distance.

"Look!" Wordsmith said, pointing. "It is the face of the Child!"

The fog and smoke had lifted for a long moment and revealed the face of the mountain to be the face of the Child—

not finely sculptured, but recognizable, though anyone determined to see no miracle would see only the crags of the rough-
hewn mountain.

Then even that resemblance faded under the mist, until it
was merely a melting mountain again—alive now with little
rivers and waterfalls tumbling down the steep sides and forming greater waters below.

They moved on.

*   *   *

Lionheart arrived in Heartshope on the run. "They have
returned!" he panted. "And a child comes with them!"

They appeared over the top of the hill just as Lionheart had
said—a child, walking happily between Wordsmith and Beauty, with Freeblade stalking proudly behind. Pacing in honor on
either side were lions and bears and deer and wolves.

SIX

The Sign
of the
Child

And now what?" asked Brightface of no one in particular.

The entire Company sat in a circle, gazing at the Child. He
ate quietly and smiled at them all.

She continued with her questions. "Is he indeed mute? Was
his voice frozen on that awful mountain?"

Wordsmith attempted an answer. "He has said nothing to
us. Remember that Covenant said there would come a time
when words would be too much, and yet not enough. Perhaps
this is what he meant."

"He sent the Child, didn't he?" asked Binder.

"He must have," said Beauty.

"Then we are not forsaken," stated Freeblade, a ring of comfort in his voice.

"Not now," replied Wordsmith, "and most likely we never
were."

The Child rose, went to Beauty and looked into her eyes while he stroked her face with his tiny hand.

"These are *his* eyes," she said, "Troubled, deep and old. He has come from Covenant."

"Is this Covenant come among us again?" asked Brightface.

"I do not know. They are very like," Beauty said. "A heart-breaking child," she murmured.

"Perhaps he is the child of a broken heart," added Brightface. "How old is he?" she asked, puzzled.

"Three? Five?" answered Wordsmith. "Perhaps age has no meaning for him. Covenant said we would be the first of all people to behold the face of the Everlasting Child—and he said there would be one who was never born and will never die."

"What shall we do if he does not speak?" asked Lionheart.

Wordsmith shook his head. "Then we must learn to listen to the words he does not say."

Freeblade spoke. "The Child, as you have seen, is helpless—without cloak, without food, without power, without speech. Yet he has a work to do, and we must care for him while he works."

"What does he need?" continued Lionheart.

"What do the other children need?" responded Brightface. "Love, food, a warm place to sleep, a world to play in . . . all these, at least, lie partly in our power." She glanced at the fire twins, who sat beside Binder curiously observing the new addition to the Company. Gazing again at the Child, she pondered, "Does he have a name?"

Beauty deferred to Wordsmith, as though they had already had such a discussion.

"If he does, we do not know it," he said.

"Perhaps we do not need to know it," Beauty added. "After all, we never knew Covenant's real name."

"That *is* his name," responded Wordsmith. "It just isn't all of it."

"I suspect this one has a magnificent name, and that 'the

Child' is merely one of them."

Though tired, they sat in the afternoon sun and watched him play with the other children—always happily, sometimes serenely, sometimes with shrieking laughter that was medicine to the hearts of the hearers.

"If the Child is happy," murmured Beauty, "then let us be happy as well."

*　*　*

Not until the Child had fallen asleep in the late afternoon did Wordsmith turn to Brightface and her news. Beauty and Freeblade joined them, listening intently to her report and gently examining the remnants of glass in the carved wooden box.

"Glory is already being torn and rebuilt at the same time," she concluded.

" 'Its destruction will be its rebuilding, and its rebuilding will be its destruction,' " quoted Wordsmith, and they remembered his voice reciting those same words around the fire.

"What does that mean?" asked Freeblade.

Wordsmith opened the little book again. "It meant nothing when we read it aloud, but perhaps we know now what it applies to. This tower does appear a pridesome thing."

"It may be beautiful when it is finished," said Beauty. "But what will it mean?"

"Candle said it was Fame's intention to see and be seen from one end of this kingdom to another."

They passed on to the glass fragments.

Wordsmith peered into the remains of the vision window while Beauty tried in vain to raise a reflection from the sliver of Covenant's magical mirror.

"Freeblade," said Wordsmith. "It is fitting that you should carry this piece of the old high window. May you see far with it, if it ever shows its magic again, for it is to you we entrust the safety of the Company."

Freeblade hesitated before replying. "But is it the safety of the Company I guard, or the safety of the Child? If I am forced to choose . . . well, you know my choice already.

"And your last protection is not me," he continued, "but Lionheart and his friends. A bevy of bears, a stand of stags, a watch of wolves—these can do more than one man with even an enchanted sword."

"Carry it anyway, please," said Wordsmith, "if for no other reason than that it pleases me."

He accepted, reluctant to bear the honor but pleased with the gift.

"The power is gone from my mirror," Beauty said to Wordsmith. "Does your glass reveal anything to you?"

Wordsmith shook his head. "No. I saw darkness there, and black swirls against it, and shadows beyond that—but no visions, no seed for stories. Even in Glory they were not created here, but here they were born and given a substance and a voice."

"Direct from the hand of the Elder God," Beauty added. "Perhaps he has another way yet to be revealed."

"Is your mirror completely dark as well?" he asked in turn.

"Not quite," she said. "All I see now is my own image, and there is no magic in seeing that."

"To some of us there is," her husband said lightly.

She squeezed his hand and turned to Freeblade. "Can you see anything there?"

"No," Freeblade answered, "though perhaps there is little to see. I do wish it could show us what is happening in Glory. How can such a place be so terribly close and so impossibly distant at the same time?"

Brightface shifted at the mention of Glory. "Wordsmith?" she asked. "I would return to Candle's house with news of the Child."

Wordsmith found no reason to deny her, so she and the boys left early that evening for Glory, the two boys riding one lion with Lionheart, while Binder and Brightface rode the other.

*   *   *

Wordsmith stayed alone that night with the Child, who sat restlessly in his lap and would neither lie down nor close his eyes.

Stirred by an old and unaccountable longing, Wordsmith began to sing softly, and at once the Child curled up in his arms. He did not even know the song himself, but the words formed for him as he sang, and he found himself singing a tale of the beggar that was well framed by the evening. By the third chorus the Child was asleep.

Wordsmith did not cease his singing, for he could no longer hold back the gift that had been silent for so long. Beauty and Freeblade heard and came to see the source of the sound; though Beauty's gaze upon his face begged him not to stop, and that same wish was echoed in Freeblade's eyes, his voice faltered and he let the song trail into silence.

But long after he himself was in bed, the music continued to echo in his head.

*   *   *

"I think," said Wordsmith to Beauty the next morning, "that Covenant's death was necessary to bring this Child among us. Nor do I think that all that has happened to us has been a surprise."

"What do you mean?"

"Covenant told me that dawn before he died that we would soon see the beginning of the dream. I asked him if he did not mean the completion of the dream, and he said no, that only now would the beginning begin.

" 'If you were to know the future all at once,' he said, 'you would not be able to bear it. You can only survive the future as it unfolds, one day at a time.' "

"Wordsmith?" Beauty whispered. "Since the Child came I have almost forgotten to grieve for Covenant, though I have not forgotten him for a moment."

"Perhaps he did not mean for us to grieve. I feel Covenant

still *is*, but that he is not anywhere we can reach him. If we could still reach him now, the Child would not have come."

His moment of brightness did not last, and he continued to return to thoughts of what had been lost. "There is no more mirror," he said sadly. "The fifth window is lifeless, and all my books are lost and . . ."

"Not all your books are lost," said Beauty. "Those you sold or gave away still have a home somewhere."

"What shall I do if I cannot write, and there is no house to be steward of?"

"You can keep loving me," suggested Beauty. "As long as we both draw breath, I am yours.

"And," she added quietly, "perhaps now it is time for you to begin singing again."

He was struck cold by the thought, and old feelings he thought long-denied rose again to the surface of his heart.

"Covenant entrusted you with his words," she said, "and you wrote them faithfully. Perhaps now it is time you laid down your pen and lifted up your voice.

"Songs need not be written down," Beauty continued, "as long as the words remain firmly in your head."

"I had not sung since the night Covenant quenched the fire we set for him and set his own fires raging through our fields," he said. "I did not have the heart to sing as my village was dying. And then Covenant took away my old songs. Since that day I have not felt worthy.

"I found joy in my stories, but now there are no more books," he said sadly.

"No room," said Beauty softly.

"No time," added Wordsmith. "You cannot write as you run."

She agreed. "But you *can* sing . . ."

"It is an old sadness," he said, "and I would rather leave it alone."

"It does seem that we will be travelers now, until another

home can be found."

"Not in Glory."

"No. Somewhere else. This is a big land."

"Not too big for Fame's men to find us."

"I am not glad we were forced to flee here," she said, "but I am glad we had this place to come to. It is not Covenant's House, nor do we have Covenant. But we have the Child, and in Heartshope we have peace. Do you think we are really safe here?"

"For now," he said.

"For long?"

"I do not know."

In the unanswerable silence they heard Brightface talking outside, and went to meet her.

"Lonely Mountain is indeed melting," she told them immediately, "and it has brought terror to Glory. Some said they saw a face in the heights, and all are uneasy at the new river that is forming from the melted ice. It has begun to flow already through what once were dry fields, and the first feelers are creeping past the walls of Glory."

"This is important," Wordsmith said, "but I do not know what it means." He wandered away to ponder his book again.

But away from the village and sitting near the orchard stream, Wordsmith could not concentrate on the words, even though they were Covenant's final words to all of them and the key to what lay ahead. Drawn by a desire he could no longer deny, yet unsure of his ability or freedom to begin singing again at will, he began to test his voice there where no one could hear.

Another song came to him unbidden and unknown, though telling a story he had long since written by hand and sold in the marketplace.

When he was done, he was startled to hear Beauty applauding behind him.

"Do not stop," she said. "Sing me another story."

"Stories?" he asked, fearful and hopeful at the same time. "Yes, I still see stories in my head, but now they burst into my mind as songs. Now how am I to cease my singing? My thoughts are always there, and the words ready at hand, and the first note of music its own spark to song."

"Do not cease, then," begged Beauty. "You would rob us all of pleasure if you denied yourself the fruit of your head and heart."

He sang for her, tentatively at first and then with power, and time ticked away unheeded.

*   *   *

After that the hours became days, and the weeks followed. Heartshope slipped into a comfortable routine, welcome after their loss and weariness. The Child did little but love and accept their love. He played, the essence of child—honest, in-nocent, but without trace of selfishness or immaturity—while absorbing the world with the understanding of a wise old man.

He said nothing to anyone, but the village was never denied his bright smile. Nor was Wordsmith's singing long absent, or Beauty's tender hand missing from anything that happened.

*   *   *

"This Child is afraid of nothing," said Binder to Freeblade, "yet he must be protected."

"Yes," said Freeblade, "though it is also a mystery to me. *This* is power," he continued, watching the Child caress Beauty's face. "While *this*," he added, waving his sword, "is only a pos-ture born of the poverty of powerlessness.

"I protect him? With the sword, if I may. But better he should protect me from the darkness of the world—the kind that cannot be defeated with a sword."

*   *   *

The Child was everywhere, always accessible, yet never plumbed by anyone who drew near him—even by those who drank of his warmth and goodness until their aches and hurts were momentarily drowned in a sweet tide of wonder.

None held him too long, for even though he gave himself freely to them they knew he was not theirs to command.

Yet none could leave him alone, for he was so serene and filled with some secret joy that others could not behold.

And that joy was contagious.

"I do not understand," said Brightface once. "I pick him up to comfort him, and yet it is he who comforts me."

Yet the Child continued to say nothing, and only smiled, beckoned and snuggled, giving as much pleasure as he received.

* * *

Freeblade, standing guard one day, realized he had not seen the lions for some time. He came in search of Lionheart and asked, "Where are your lions and wolves and wild friends?"

"I do not know," replied Lionheart. "They have all vanished. Nor have I seen any animals at all since yesterday. Hear for yourself."

They listened, and heard nothing. No birds sang. Nothing moved in the trees or disturbed the silence of the brush.

SEVEN

Trouble
and
Travail

THE EVENING HAD ALREADY BEGUN TO DEEPEN AROUND Heartshope when Freeblade emerged from the trees and sought Wordsmith. "A man is coming," he reported. "A man, walking alone. He has left the road to Glory and is coming this way."

"Do we know him?" asked Wordsmith.

"I cannot tell in the dusk. He has stopped twice to rest and more often to look, as though he is not sure where he is going."

"Are there others behind him?"

Freeblade shook his head. "Not to my knowledge."

"Let us go and see."

"Where is the Child?" Freeblade asked.

"Brightface is with him in the house, and the last time I looked, they had both fallen asleep."

Freeblade was content, and the two left Heartshope behind. Soon they crept past the lepers' graveyard and stopped behind a rock.

"Over there, beneath that pair of trees," whispered Free-blade.

"Where? I see nothing."

"There is nothing to see unless you know he is there. He makes much noise when he moves, but at rest he is very, very still."

As they quietly drew near, a shadow detached itself from the darker shadows and moved toward them.

"Halt!" cried Freeblade.

No one moved, no one breathed for two long heartbeats.

"Freeblade?" asked the stranger weakly.

"I know that voice. Is that Candle?" he countered.

"It is," came the reply. "And Wordsmith?"

Freeblade lowered his sword. "Are you alone?"

"Yes."

"Welcome to Heartshope," the warrior said, and they closed the last few steps between them to embrace.

"I would not have come like this," began Candle, "unannounced in the dark, but I could not wait any longer to speak with you."

"Are you all right? Is there trouble?" Wordsmith asked anxiously.

"Yes, we are all right, for now. But I don't know how much longer we will be safe in Glory. We need your help."

"Name it," said Wordsmith. "And if it is in our power we will grant it gladly."

"We have decided to leave Glory—and soon."

"I will make sure he was not followed," muttered Freeblade. He slipped away into the night.

"Let us go on to Heartshope," suggested Wordsmith. "We are safe enough here, but we can have food and a fire instead of hunger and darkness."

"And I would see the Child as well," replied Candle.

"He deserves to be seen," answered Wordsmith. "All the world should come to wonder."

"I am uneasy in Glory," Candle continued, as he and Wordsmith began to pick their way through the starlit night. "I have never seen a people so gripped by anything or anyone. Fame has them enthralled, and I do not know where it will end."

"All this in little more than two months?" Wordsmith asked.

Candle nodded. "He knows the holes in their hearts as well as in their heads, and has told them what they want to hear. 'Great is Glory!' he has called to them, and 'Great is Glory!' is the answer they give him back."

They walked on for a few measures in a silence that echoed the stillness of the sky, now quiet in the absence of the bats and owls that normally ruled the night.

"But I am more concerned about something else," Candle continued. "Moonflower does, indeed, seem to be the only woman in Glory with child, and I fear for her for that reason.

"What is different is always hated, and those who have what others desire but cannot attain are hated even more. Hard stares have come Moonflower's way, and I agree with Trueteller that Glory may no longer be safe.

"Fame has already begun to claim that good has come on his account, and may be reckoned to his reign, while he blames all the evil upon Covenant. Earthquakes, barrenness, the melting of Lonely Mountain, accidents at the Tower—all these are the beggar's fault. Your names have been mentioned as well, not directly by Fame but by those who knew the Company. If word of us three in Glory has not yet come to Fame, it soon will, and I do not wish to be found within those walls."

He paused. "Is this a wise thing, Wordsmith? You said it was good that we stayed behind, that we would know what took place in Glory."

Wordsmith thought for a few moments as they walked. "I gave no order that you stay. It was not a good time for you to travel, and I did not know the depth of our danger." He waved ahead of them, and Candle drew his first glimpse of Heartshope. "Come join us, then, as soon as you can."

"If we are to travel at all, Moonflower must travel now," he said. "She is no longer ill in the mornings, but she is growing far more rapidly than we expected, and is so swollen that we cannot easily disguise her now.

"I have sold most everything in my shop," he continued, "and have bought nothing more. I am as free to leave Glory now as I ever have been. I own little now, except bags of gold and coppers too heavy to carry."

"You need Kingsburro," Wordsmith said.

Candle nodded. "And perhaps Roadreeler as well. I miss him and would gladly work with him again."

They walked into the inner square of Heartshope.

"Lionheart should be awake by now," Wordsmith said. "He guards us throughout the night, and sleeps much during the day."

They roused Lionheart and told him of their needs.

"We can wake others," said Wordsmith. "Take as many helpers as you need."

"I will endanger no one else," replied Candle. "I need only the good beasts for a good burden."

Freeblade returned, stepping into the shrouded firelight. "He was not followed," he said, and turned his attention to his main charge. "Is the Child still asleep?" he asked anxiously. "I disliked leaving him, but . . ."

Wordsmith waved his worry away with one hand. "If he were not well, Brightface would have let it be known by now." Turning to Candle he said, "Go with Freeblade and gaze upon the face of the Child. I will see that the animals are brought without delay."

* * *

Candle had few words when Wordsmith saw him again.

"Covenant was worth dying for," was all he would say.

"Now I know that the Child is too."

Roadreeler, eager to be ridden again by Candle, pawed impatiently at the ground. The ever-patient Kingsburro sampled the grass as he waited.

Lionheart laced the ties on his battered boots. "We will range about you as far as the gates, and wait for you. Do not be afraid, but do not linger."

"Thank you," said Candle.

"Perhaps it is best if you leave by another gate," said Wordsmith, "and then come across the fields and the meadows to Heartshope from behind. If anyone sees you leave, they will not be certain you have come this way."

"You will not see me," promised Lionheart, "but I will be there." He walked ahead and was gone.

Candle, riding Roadreeler and leading Kingsburro, followed quickly.

The darkness swallowed them all.

Wordsmith returned to his house in hope of both sleep and sleeping Beauty, but Freeblade paced the edges of the village to keep awake and wait for Lionheart's return.

* * *

Trueteller entered Heartshope first, alone on Kingsburro, bulging saddlebags partially hidden beneath her flowing skirt. Candle, seated on Roadreeler and protecting Moonflower in his arms, followed her out of the darkness.

"We are here," said Candle simply. "We brought what riches we could."

"The greatest riches are the blessings we haven't yet seen," said Brightface, helping Moonflower away to the abandoned house set aside for them.

They were interrupted by the appearance of the Child.

Moonflower knelt to him, and the Child came to her and touched her belly ever so softly. Her child leaped within her for the first time, and old words leaped in Wordsmith's mind at the same moment. Then there came a second leap beside the first, and Moonflower gasped in suprise and understanding. "Twins?" she exclaimed. "No wonder I have grown so large already!"

" 'These children shall be born in the City,' " Wordsmith pronounced, his voice sounding much like the Covenant he quoted. " 'And no child will be born from now until the City is revealed.' " He paused and looked thoughtfully at Moonflower. "Once more the rumors and the promises have come together and brought forth understanding."

EIGHT

The Sign
of the
Eagle

TRUETELLER WAS EXPLORING THE VILLAGE THE NEXT MORNING
and did not see the eagle swoop from the sky until it swished
close past her head, dropped something in the grass and
soared into the air again.

"Farsight?" she called out shakily.

The eagle turned in midclimb and arrowed down to her
again, his wings cracking the air as he slowed to settle on her
outstretched arm. She stroked his feathers and murmured to
him lovingly, wincing at his claws but most happy to see him
again.

"Where have you *been?*" she asked him with soft fierceness.
Turning her head away, she called to the others. "Farsight is
here! Come and see!"

They came, and saw, and asked questions she had no
answers for.

"Where did he come from?"

"How did he find you here?"

"I do not know," she admitted, "but wherever he has been, he has come to me again."

She remembered the bands of gold, and looked; they were gone. Tears came unbidden, for Covenant's memories were suddenly very strong and sweet, and the weight of unanswered prayers and unfulfilled hopes returned to her shoulder

"He is an old promise to me," she said simply. She opened her mouth to say more, and said nothing instead.

She blinked away the tears. *What did he drop?* she wondered, and nudged the toe of her sandal through the drifted leaves and sticks on the ground.

The other people, happy for her, but with other thoughts on their minds, went back to their labors.

Something round and purple rolled away from her foot. *Of course,* she thought, *a cavada fruit. Where did he find it?* It was still fairly fresh and firm, though marked by his claws, as though he had carried it a long distance.

She carefully moved Farsight onto her arm, stooped, picked up the fruit, brushed the dirt away and offered it to him. He ate greedily. "Are you hungry?" she asked him. "You must have come a long way."

But when she offered him anything else, he refused. After that, he seemed restless.

And within the hour he was gone again.

Trueteller watched his silhouette fade away to the south.

*   *   *

She was delighted when Farsight returned to her again the next morning, bearing more fruit.

"What is that?" asked one of the children.

"Cavada," Trueteller replied. "Some people call them frost-berries. When Farsight was wounded, I tried to find something he would eat. Candle had these in his shop, and Farsight liked them. I guess he has found a place where they grow."

"Why does he bring them to you?"

Trueteller shrugged. "Who knows? He could eat them himself, but he seems to prefer them from my hand. I certainly don't mind."

After that, he returned again and again, at shorter intervals, and staying only a few moments each time.

"What is he doing?" asked Freeblade. "Where is he finding all the frostfruit?"

"I wish I knew," she said, watching him wing away into the dusk. *I know nothing at all,* she thought, *but I can always hope for everything.*

* * *

"Trueteller?" called Beauty.

"Yes?" she answered, pulling weeds from between the uneven rows of vegetables.

"Farsight has returned again."

"I do not think he strays far from us now," said Trueteller, not looking up from her work.

"But this time he's not alone," said Beauty.

Trueteller, rising, saw Farsight on the shoulder of a strange and rugged man, ragged from the road and ruined by a lifetime of labor. Oddly, he was staring at her, and not at Beauty. She looked again, inhaled sharply, and nearly fell.

"I know that man," she said so quietly only Beauty heard her. "Time, toil and tears cannot disguise him."

Beauty's heart began to pound, her instinct outracing her knowledge.

Farsight leaped into the air and wheeled over their heads.

"Darmak?" Trueteller asked.

"Abra?" the man asked in return.

Weeds and work forgotten, Trueteller stumbled to him. She nearly disappeared in his grasp, her face crushed into his shaggy shoulder, one of his massive hands cradling the back of her head.

"This is Darmak," she finally said to Beauty, after the

stunned silence. She almost kept a waver out of her voice. "He is my husband."

All of them began to cry.

This moment is only for two, thought Beauty. Farsight circled overhead as she withdrew to the village to find Wordsmith and wait.

* * *

When Trueteller brought Darmak into Heartshope, the rest were waiting expectantly—Candle and Moonflower in front, with Wordsmith, Beauty, Freeblade and the Child standing behind them.

"This is Darmak, my husband," Trueteller said, her voice still trembling around the edges. She held out in her palm a twisted gold band. "He is Covenant's final promise to me."

She beckoned Moonflower forward. "This is your child, Darmak," she continued, "and inside her are your child's children."

Moonflower took his hand shyly.

"I never knew we had a child," he marveled.

"Yet she is bone of your bone and blood of your blood. Unknowing, you left her with me when you . . . disappeared."

"I don't know what to say," Moonflower murmured.

"Nor do I," answered Darmak. "Except that you are your mother again as I first beheld her; I would have known you anywhere as hers." An awkward silence fell for a moment.

"Go on with your life, Moonflower," he eventually said. "We will be friends in time, for a gap of twenty years cannot be leaped with a single bound."

Candle stepped forward to stand beside her. "And this is Candle," said Trueteller. "Moonflower is his now, and he is hers."

"Moonflower? Candle?" Darmak queried. "A pair of unusual names."

"The story behind those names is far more than unusual, and they call me Trueteller now."

"Who does?" Darmak asked.

"Covenant did, first," she answered, "and then the rest, after."

"Covenant?"

She held out the band again. "The man who gathered these people together, who bade me hammer this gold for you."

"I still do not understand."

Wordsmith spoke. "Trueteller is, indeed, her name now, and she has much truth to tell you."

"This is Wordsmith," Trueteller continued, "with Beauty, and Freeblade our defender. They lead us, now that Covenant is gone. And this is the Child."

"Whose child?" he asked.

Trueteller hesitated. "It's hard to say," she finally answered.

Darmak's confusion deepened.

"We welcome you among us," said Wordsmith with a hint of awkward formality, "but your place is with your wife now. She has much to tell you and much to hear. We will not disturb you until you wish to see us again. We will come to know you later."

"But for now, Trueteller," Beauty suggested, "take him away and enjoy him. You have waited twenty years for this day."

"Go on," urged Freeblade. "We will see that your work is done for you."

The two walked away, and Trueteller steered her husband toward the orchards and the soft riverbank.

"Are you hungry?" she asked him, belatedly.

He nodded. "For many things," he answered, "but not for food. It will take time to set things right again."

"I did not even know if you were alive," she said.

"I did not know if you had married another, or if you even still thought of me," he replied.

"I have thought of no one *but* you."

For a while no words would come. After that, the words

would not cease flowing, and eventually no words were enough. Where the waters curled around the trees, the two found a half-shaded place to sit.

She helped ease his weathered cloak from his tired shoulders, and ran her fingers gently along the small scars there. Then she showed him her own shoulders, with like marks from the same claws.

"These shoulders were not made for eagles," he said ruefully, though without sadness.

"Or else this eagle was not made for shoulders," she countered. "But his place was there for a time and a purpose—and we have adapted quite well now, haven't we?" she added. "These shall all be ancient scars some day."

He worked his back against a tree and made a nest for her in his arms.

"I scarcely remember how to love you," he said.

She sighed and made herself even more comfortable in his embrace. "You have forgotten nothing so far," she whispered.

NINE

Wildhaven

THE MORNING IN HEARTSHOPE WAS QUIET UNTIL BINDER STOOD from his labors and gazed around.

"Look!" he cried, sweeping his arm from one side to the other.

Those near him looked up from their work too.

Heartshope was completely and silently surrounded. On every side, on every patch of ground and every tree limb, animals waited and watched, making no sound.

"Lionheart!" called Binder. "Come see! The animals have come back to Heartshope."

Lionheart emerged from his house, rubbing sleep from his eyes, and was surprised. The animals watched him closely, though there was no menace in their eyes.

"Wherever they were," Lionheart finally agreed, "they are, indeed, here now."

Wordsmith and Beauty came from their house and were also surprised. The Child came behind them and smiled. He did not seem surprised.

Then the animals turned their gaze to the Child and came to him from all sides—a flood of fur and feathers that halted crouching before him, their wild but unwavering eyes fixed hopefully upon the small boy with the ancient eyes.

Delighted, the Child beamed upon them, and caressed the muzzles and beaks nearest him; content, he pointed to Lionheart and stepped back from the gathering. The beasts' gazes swiveled toward Lionheart again.

As though waiting only for the right moment, the largest lion rose and nudged Lionheart affectionately—but so firmly that he fell across the animal's back and was forced to straddle the shaggy back to keep from falling. The lion shouldered him into place and at once began to shamble off toward the trees. The other animals followed after. Startled, Lionheart thwacked the lion vainly with his palm, yelling and roaring alternately without effect.

"The Child is smiling," called Wordsmith. "Go with the animals, and fear not."

"An easy thing to say," retorted Lionheart, smiling in spite of himself. "You are not surrounded."

Remembering the frosty night on the mountain when the beasts came, Wordsmith called out, "But I have been! And this is more of the same sort of magic!"

They watched the soft procession pace, stalk, wriggle, hop and fly from sight, taking all the natural sound of the wild with it. No birds remained to sing, no beetles stayed to scrape, no squirrels tarried to thunder in the underbrush.

When Wordsmith thought to look again, he saw the unconcerned Child building new kingdoms in the dirt.

* * *

Wordsmith and Beauty and the rest heard Lionheart's return long before they saw him.

An amazing series of chirps, groans, growls, hiccoughs, tweets and hoots echoed through the woods, and then Lionheart entered Heartshope, bringing a vast shadow behind him. All the animals trailed in his wake, and this time they were not silent but joyful, voicing all manner of sounds and music.

Then they collapsed around Lionheart's feet, stilling temporarily, and Lionheart spoke. "I certainly do not understand this," he announced dazedly, "and can scarcely believe. Ever since the City was lost, the animals have been waiting for me to come." He shook his head, as though the new reality still were not clear to him. "They knew that Covenant had come to the land. They were waiting for him, and he bid them wait for the man who would gather them all in safety, a man who would save them."

"And you are that man?" asked Freeblade.

"I must be," Lionheart shrugged. "No one knows another answer.

"He showed the animals this place—Heartshope—and told them to watch here for the man who rode the lions. They knew my identity before even I did, from the first time I was privileged to sit astride. But they had to wait until I came *here*."

"Do you then command this army?" asked Freeblade.

"No," he answered immediately. "They will help us, and we will help them, but they are not here at my beck and call. Remember that *they* summoned *me*," he added.

"And now what do they want?"

"The same gifts we do. Health. Hope. Freedom. Innocence. Peace."

"How do you talk with them?" wondered Beauty.

"I cannot teach you to hear their words or share their thoughts, for I did not learn myself: it was a gift given to me for a purpose.

"They hunger, they fear, they love, they thirst," Lionheart said, "but they do not think like us or communicate in the same way. It is difficult to describe how they share their thoughts. They think in pictures and emotions, and talk in images—what they saw, where they saw it, when it was seen.

"I sense the image in their minds, and I can feel the fear or the warmth that they bring with it, but they cannot always tell me what it means. They do not understand human minds, though they are learning again to know our hearts since Covenant came.

"Covenant," he continued. "They have hundreds of images of Covenant. When he was not with us, he must have been with them, leaving promises with them. After what I have seen, I would not be surprised if Covenant had spoken to the rocks and trees as well. It seems he was as concerned for this entire world as he was for us."

He paused. "None of this is very clear, you realize, and we can talk of it later. This is a new and unexpected gift, and I'm still learning what its powers are."

He gestured to the waiting animals. "They are not our natural enemies, and need not be our enemies at all. We and the animals were meant to be on the same side. We are enemies with them only because we are our own worst enemies.

"Nor were the animals themselves always at war with one another, though not one of these hunters is innocent of his prey's blood. They are bound to this law of tooth and claw, and suffer in its chains.

"They will help us, if they can. But they also need our help, and I do not know whose need will be the stronger. They suffer with us, and because of us," he said, "and I cannot turn them away. I cannot proclaim peace forever, but I can call an end to that war in this place.

"We have marked out the land around Heartshope, from the road to Glory on the west to the peaks of the low mountains on the east, from the fields to the north to the next river to the south.

"There shall be no more killing, for hunger or in anger, in all this protected territory. Let them eat not each other but the yield of the field and the fruit of the trees." He smiled, and singled out Trueteller with his words. "So they were all once, Trueteller. Your eagle is less unusual than you believed."

She laughed, and he turned to them all again. "They have each pledged to harm nothing that lives and moves, and you need fear nothing from them. I have not pledged that you would not harm them, but I promised that you would give your answer yourselves."

"Who objects?" asked Wordsmith of the Company.

No voices were heard.

"Then let it be," he said quietly. He turned to the multitude of animals. "Welcome to the Company of Covenant," he told them, as though they could understand his words. "Where the Child opens his arms, we open our arms as well."

Lionheart resumed his speech. "I would name this area the kingdom of Wildhaven, with Heartshope its great center.

"The animals everywhere will be told, and they must choose between their old war outside Wildhaven and this new peace within."

"Hail, Lionheart—Beastmaster!" intoned Wordsmith.

Lionheart laughed, and then saw that Wordsmith had meant no joke. An awkward expression bloomed on his face and then faded into contentment. "It seems I must accept that title. But it is not I who brings this harmony," he reminded them. "Rejoice, but know that it is not Lionheart's doing. It is a gift to us—from Covenant, from the Child, perhaps direct from the hand of the Elder God."

* * *

There were animals everywhere in Heartshope. Squirrels skittered across the square, ignored by the hawks gliding in and out among the trees. Lions sprawled in the square, twitching slightly but not rousing when rabbits ran across their outstretched paws. Wolf cubs played at Roadreeler's feet while he grazed the grass.

"This is amazing," commented Wordsmith.

"Not so amazing as the Child," replied Beauty. "He must be the source of this harmony. Without him, there would be nothing like this."

She sighed, and Wordsmith asked her what was wrong.

"I was only wondering," she answered, "why people could not live together like this as well."

"Perhaps they will," said Wordsmith. "I have a feeling the Child has only begun his work among us."

*　*　*

"All the game is gone," muttered an old man hunting in the woods far from Heartshope. "I do not understand it."

TEN

The Secret Place

WORDSMITH?" ASKED TRUETELLER. "I HAVE HEARD DARMAK'S story now, and I think all should hear it. Could we all share a fire tonight and let him speak?"

"Of course!" he responded. "Promises and miracles, of all things, should not be kept secret."

* * *

Darmak started speaking easily, even eagerly.

"I have waited a long time to tell this story," he began, looking at them all but most often at Trueteller.

"You know that Abra—Trueteller—and I lived in the woods, a place that was our home and our living as well. As I had done so many times before, I gathered from the forest all I could carry—mushrooms, berries, roots, herbs, choice woods—anything that another might buy or trade for. And as had happened before, the farther I walked from the forests, the more coppers I was offered for my gleanings, for such things as I had were not common there.

"Two men asked me to bring my forest fare to the far south, where everything I took for granted would be considered delicacies indeed.

"Though they were strangers, I journeyed with them suspecting nothing, while listening to their tales of a rare wilderness fruit called *cavada*.

"We detoured to see the place where the fruit grew, and I found all their words true. A deep, cold valley amid impossible heights—endless pale sunshine, and ever the deep drifts of snow. It grows on great bushy trees that line the trackless faces of the cliffs, waiting only for the hands to pack it in cartons lined with dry hay. More cavada grows in that valley than can readily be picked, for the land is rugged and remote, weather-blown and treacherous. None would stay long for harvest unless they were desperate—or enslaved.

"And that, I discovered too late, is exactly how they were gathered—by slaves.

"My companions quickly became my captors, and shoved me down a long and unclimbable slope into the valley. I found other men down there before me, and learned more of my fate.

"Our task was to pick the cavada. Our choices were simple and unavoidable: we could work and be fed, or rebel and die. At the cliff they could haul the baskets of fruit up and lower food and clothing down to us, or give us wood suited for fire or shelter.

"Never has the gap between one person and another seemed greater.

"The valley was huge, and we constantly explored for a way out. We fashioned ropes for ourselves—needing them, indeed, for our work—but we had nothing to fasten them to and, therefore, no way to climb over the cliffs that kept us captive.

If one of us could have reached the top of the cliffs, he could have let longer ropes down to the rest.

"A way of escape was clear, and before our eyes every waking moment, but impossible. We could not reach the escape we saw, and we could see no other escape within our reach."

He paused, and they could see him trying to find the right thread in all the thoughts tangled together in his mind. Freeblade stretched out his foot and nudged a stray log back into the fire.

"The years wore on," Darmak resumed, "and though the frostberries were delicacies in all the land, we quickly grew tired of them. They were always there, rotting underfoot, and though we ate them to live we came to despise the fruit that delighted the world.

"Men came and men died. Most perished quickly, for the mountains were unforgiving, and they were soon conquered by the cliffs. Others chose the plunge into an abyss over slavery.

"Our captors cared not; they had ample chances to steal other men to replace the careless, the sick and the defiant.

"We had no hope at all. How could anyone outside know? The mountains kept their cold secrets too well.

"I was the only one who lasted twenty years. The rest were young and hot and reckless, full of anger and smoke and impatience. I was young and cold and determined, and did not let my anger drive me vainly.

"I went farther and farther into the valley for my labors, preferring the solitude to the company of other wretched men. One day I discovered a very old and sacred place in the cliffs. It was tiny, and held only an altar with the name of the Elder God upon it, and a mark I did not recognize. Once the hidden nook had been an open place, but rocks had fallen, the land had slid, and time had erased the path, as well as any reasons for its presence there.

"What do prisoners think of except escape? Through the

years I held the cold fire in my belly, burning for freedom and revenge, and in that secret place I prayed for both. But none of my prayers were heard until I grew tired of anger and learned to cease to long for blood. When I sought escape only, I found peace at that altar—and eventually an answer came.

"An answer that came from the air.

"There were always animals in that place, and we watched for them. There were bears, and we never interrupted them in their feeding. There were foxes too, even wolves. We trapped some smaller animals to add to the food so grudgingly given us, and to use their furs to warm us against the wind.

"I saw an eagle in the air one day, and I ignored it, for it was only one of countless birds that came day by day for the feast of fruit. But it settled near me and made raucous noises at me—pestering me for food, trying to snatch the cavada from my hand as I picked it, ignoring that which was still on the trees or already fallen to the ground. I finally tossed him some fruit to be rid of him.

"But then I saw the gold bands on his legs, and my head grew light. I saw your mark, Abra . . . and I could not wait to tame him enough to pry the bands from him and see what other message lay inside.

"And the second mark? That mark was the same as that on the altar in the secret place.

"I could only make wild guesses where he had come from or who had tamed him, or how he had come by both your mark and this sign connected to the Elder God.

"I called him 'Featherfriend,' " he said. "That at least goes well with Farsight.

"In the end, which of us befriended the other? You cannot know, for I can never put into words how much he cheered me and brought me hope of a world I thought had left me behind forever.

"I know now it was Trueteller who first showed him kindness, who tended to him and gave him his taste for cavada. He stayed with me, insisting on keeping me in sight and eating only from my hand, and I began to see him as not only a messenger but a rescuer.

"He readily plucked fruit from the higher branches and brought it to me, halving my labor for each full sack, even though he later gobbled much of what he brought me.

"From there, it was not difficult to persuade Featherfriend to retrieve bundles of rope on command. I don't think I trained him, but he agreed to help me. And next I tied a loop in a long rope and offered it to Featherfriend. He caught it in his beak and flew off up the rock and lodged it around a stone spur. Then he wheeled in the air while I climbed the rock and stood triumphant there.

"So I discovered a chance of freedom, and we practiced where the others could not watch. I wove strong ropes, long ropes, more than I could possibly carry, for I had an idea. I began to hoard my food and wrap it well against the elements and the mice."

He paused and let several clouds pass over the moon before he spoke again. "But that was not my greatest struggle. I fought myself daily whether I should take the others with me. Yet we could not all go. If we all had vanished, they might have looked for us and found us pinned halfway up the cliffs. Nor could I doubt that the others would have chosen to return in force and kill our captors.

"In the end, I took none with me. But I left a marker for the others, if they looked for me, and I left the ropes in place for the brave. They can follow, if they wish.

"Unpursued, Featherfriend and I found a way across the mountain—trackless, undiscovered, even more hazardous than the valley. From rock to rock he led me, bringing ropes and carrying the ends ever higher, waiting while I fought every foot of the climb, bringing me fruit throughout the journey. The way was dizzy, and perilous, but I had ceased to fear by then—except to fear that I would not return to this place again.

"We gained the summit, and passed on into the forests where I finally fell and lay for days, and he brought me not only fruit but fish and rabbits to share.

"Later we found the road again—and encountered one of my captors returning from a trip. At first he was surprised, then angry, for I would not tell him how I came there.

"I could not plead my freedom, but I could claim it, and in the end I could pay gold to keep it. He agreed to believe that I had fallen into the crevasses—if I gave him the gold band."

He hesitated. "I did not know which band to give him. In the end, I gave him the one with the strange mark upon it. I knew your work, Abra, and I wished to carry it with me.

"It is no longer complete," he continued sadly. "I have had to hammer off other bits along the way, to buy shelter and food."

"It does not matter," Trueteller sighed, dismissing the thought with a glowing smile. "The gold matters less than the man who returns it to me.

Darmak grasped her hand and continued. "I saw in his eyes that he considered killing me and taking all my gold—but seeing Featherfriend, he dared not. With this proud beast on my shoulder, I walked away from him.

"He had his choice. He could say nothing, or he could raise a cry after me. Whether he has kept silence or not, I do not know. If any followed my path, either captive or captor, they have not found me.

"Hoping all things and expecting nothing, I returned to our house in the forest, and I found only an empty shell. But there were notches at the open door, and marks I knew too well.

"For the third time I beheld that mark—first in the secret place, second on the gold band and now in the ruins of my own house. And I would have followed that mark straight to Glory, but Featherfriend drew me aside from the road, and . . . you know what happened then."

He looked at Trueteller again. "And when my explanations were done, she had many things to explain to me. What was this mark? How did it come to be beside hers? Why did I find it also at our house in the forest? Why have I encountered it at every turning since?"

Wordsmith asked him, "And are you content with her answers?"

"I am," he responded, "for now." With that he ran out of words, at last, and let silence fall unhindered.

The fire was also content in its crackling, and an easy calm had replaced the anticipation and curiosity on the faces around the fire.

"I will never eat of that fruit again," pledged Candle, his voice sliding into the silence without shattering it. "Any more that come my way I will feed to Featherfriend."

"Nor will I," agreed Trueteller, "even though that cavada from your store brought us together again." She turned again to her husband. "I am pained to think that so many of our coppers and coins went to enforce your slavery."

She gazed at the eagle, upright on a nearby tree limb with his head tucked under his wing. "I called him Farsight," she continued. "You have added to that good name another—Farsight Featherfriend."

"Is not this the way for all of us?" asked Wordsmith. "The more good we do, the more names we receive."

Beauty's voice joined his. "We have all been given, or have taken, names that are ours, but not ours forever."

"I had not heard my name for twenty years," Darmak said uncomfortably, "save in my dreams. But I have spoken her name to myself so often, and now I cannot grow used to calling her Trueteller, even though I know her story now."

"Covenant has—had—a custom," Trueteller answered for them all, "of giving new names wherever he had given new hope. He spoke to me often of his promises, and on two occasions he murmured a single name: Skymarker. He would not tell me what it meant, except that it would have much meaning for me. I think he intended to pass this name to you. Before I heard your story, the name meant nothing to me, but now I see the perfect fit."

"Perhaps my old name does not fit me now," he consented.

"With your permission, then," she said, "let us call you Skymarker. We can grow used to our new names together."

"Together," said Skymarker after a silence. "That was my grand hope all those years."

"It is no longer a hope, but reality now," she answered.

"I have been thinking," he said, "about that reality renewed. We were poor, and never had pledges. Perhaps we should use this last bit of gold to fashion anew what we never had."

"Gladly," she said. "After all, I have already worked that metal once. It was a hard and painful task, but labor shared will be twice as easy and far more enjoyable."

Someone yawned and another moved tiredly.

Binder spoke out for the first time that night, looking very thoughtful indeed. "Trueteller," he said, "there is something you should know, and something the rest may wish to hear, for it has the smile of Covenant hidden in it."

"Go on," she urged.

"When you were tending Farsight in Glory, I wondered at the name *cavada*, and I searched an old book for its meaning."

"And?"

"Have you noticed how it sounds like 'Covenant'?"

She nodded.

"It comes from the same word," he continued. "Simply put, the cavada is the promise fruit. The name meant nothing to me then."

"It means everything to me now," she said, her eyes shining even brighter.

*　*　*

"The years have been lifted from her shoulders overnight,"

remarked Wordsmith to Beauty as everyone drifted off to their homes.

"Twenty, to be exact," she murmured, taking his hand. "I'm glad we haven't had to wait that long."

ELEVEN

Encounter
at
Evening

OVER THE NEXT FEW WEEKS THE LINES OF SLEEPLESSNESS and worry largely faded from Freeblade's face. Where once he had measured the length and the breadth of the long, dark nights with his weary strides, now there were animals in abundance to watch and warn and guard. Although he woke often and still patrolled the fields and border streams, he was glad to surrender his tiredness to the night hours like all the others in Heartshope.

Another month behind us, and still we are safe, he thought. *But what will happen next?* He thought of the Child. *I was called to defend him, but defend him against what? Who would come against him? The Child receives the adoration and loyalty of each person who beholds him. Who else in all the land, except Fame, could be counted his enemy?*

* * *

Brightface journeyed once more to Glory and returned with

the sum of what she had heard in the marketplace and seen in the streets.

"Glory is firmly Fame's now," she reported sadly. "He holds the people with the power of lies. First he taught them lies about himself, and when they believed those he told them lies about themselves. He is great, he tells them, and because he is great they will all be great.

"The Mountain still melts, and the river flows past the edge of Glory, making its way to the sea. Fame claims credit for what he says is the fruit of his magic.

"It is no longer a tower that Fame builds, but the Tower. And with the fever of his lies, it grows—for the greater glory of Glory."

"Yet nothing is happening here," said Freeblade almost mournfully. "Time passes. Our enemy grows stronger. And still we do nothing."

"We do nothing because the Child has done nothing," answered Wordsmith.

"Much is happening here in Heartshope," added Beauty, "and each day. Moonflower grows and glows. More animals come, and the ones that are here grow bolder and tamer with us. Vegetables sprout in the gardens. Thankfully, even faster than the weeds. Fruits ripen in the orchards and drop into our hands."

"You know what I mean," insisted Freeblade. "That book of Covenant's words to us is full of war and warnings, while we have seen little to be wary of."

Wordsmith frowned. "There will be enough of that eventually," he promised. "None of his words were uttered lightly. Are you that anxious to fight again?"

Freeblade shook his head firmly. "I am not anxious to fight, but to win and have done with it. If there is no more fighting ever, I will be more than content. But I am not patient enough to wait long for what must come."

* * *

We've grown used to this so quickly, thought Beauty, stepping around a sleeping bear. *Nothing like this has ever happened before—anywhere—and we have come to take it for granted.*

She was hardly aware that another sparrow had landed on her shoulder.

* * *

The Child slept where he wished, often with Beauty and Wordsmith, other times with Binder and Brightface, and sometimes cushioned amid a heap of Lionheart's charges.

His fascination had quickly extended to Candle and Trueteller and Moonflower.

"I do not know whether to cradle him in my arms or worship him," said Candle one day.

"If you were a mother," replied Trueteller, "you would know how to do both at the same time."

* * *

But Freeblade always knew where the Child was and never wandered far away.

"When the Child sleeps, I am content," he murmured to Beauty one night as they watched the Child, asleep in Trueteller's arms.

"When he wakes, I am even more content," answered Beauty. They watched him silently, and secretly blessed the peace that had fallen on them.

But in the dark stillness came a silent movement at the door, and Lionheart interrupted them quietly. "Soldiers are near," he whispered. "Farsight has seen them. A band of ten, perhaps, off the main road to the south. Two miles away, no more. What shall we do?"

"Are they searching for us?" Freeblade asked.

"It may not matter. They are perilously close to finding us anyway."

"Take your beasts and frighten them away if you can."

"Some of my little friends should be there by now. But will a dozen armed men be routed by a few wild animals?"

"Either forced back, or drawn aside. But do not kill anyone, or let our own be hurt, unless there is no other way." Freeblade drew his sword. "Remember, they will have not only swords and knives but also spears and arrows. Do not get too close. I will go out beyond the village and wait. If you cannot stop them, I will."

"How?"

"It is not for show that I have kept this blade sharp and ready." He paused only long enough to run his thumb along the edge of his weapon. "Beauty," he said, "have Wordsmith smother the fires, then come after us. Stay with all the children, and quiet them if they wake.

"Trueteller, stay here with the Child, and yield the door to none but me. He is asleep, and I will not waken him unless we are forced to flee."

Lionheart plunged ahead and was soon lost in the darkness.

Freeblade followed more slowly. *Why am I protecting the Child?* he thought again. *He has more power, and more life, than I do.* He stopped in the gathering gloom of the concealing forest and waited against hope for the men to come. *Veer away,* he thought. *Do not make us spill blood over innocence.*

Eventually he heard them. Soldiers they may have been, but woodsmen they were not. Their stumbling thunder grew, and then faded away in the trees to his right. They were drawing near the main road again and would miss the evidence of Heartshope.

But Freeblade soon heard someone else coming through the forest directly before him. Not Lionheart, not an animal, but a lone soldier groping in the dark. The faint clink of metal weapons and the rattle of a full quiver betrayed him.

Freeblade's sword twitched unbidden in his hand, and the stray gleam of moonlight on metal halted his opponent.

Both were ready, and their fight began with a fierce clash of steel. Satisfaction thrilled through Freeblade's veins, for in the first slashes and parries he knew his half-seen opponent.

He had met those same strokes in the arena only weeks past, and he vividly remembered every rough moment of that encounter.

But now it was dark, no one was there to cheer him, and his opponent was wiser. Freeblade blocked, struck, drew blood, blocked again, tempted his foe into an off-balance swing and sliced hard at the hand that held the sword. A smothered shriek lost itself in the darkness, and his opponent wavered.

Freeblade struck again, and one more time.

* * *

Wordsmith joined Freeblade over the fallen soldier's form.

"What did you do to him?" whispered Wordsmith, watching the shadows for other enemies.

"I did not wish to kill him," panted Freeblade. "Nor could I let him go to bear the sword against us later. And I could not let him defeat me, for the peril of the Child." Haunted eyes stared out from his pale face.

"What *did* you do?"

"I remembered the tournament, knowing also that this man was both my opponent and the enemy of the Child. So I slashed the sword from his hand, striking off his fingers. Then I knocked his legs from beneath him, and at last brought the haft down on his head. His leg is only broken, and his head and hand and side will heal, but he will never bear the sword again."

He sighed deeply, finding it hard to select the necessary words. "I did not kill him, but I wounded him gravely. Now he is our prisoner, but I do not know what to do with him. I do not even know if I made the right decision."

"I believe," said Wordsmith slowly, "that compassion is always the right decision."

Freeblade listened carefully to the night. "Has Lionheart returned?"

"No."

"I do not hear the rest. Did he draw them away?"

They waited until the silhouette of a man on a lion appeared at the edge of the woods.

"They are gone," said Lionheart.

"Not all of them," said Freeblade, gesturing to the battered body at his feet. "This one was separated from the rest."

"We will look again," said Lionheart, "and see that no more are missing from their number."

"Did you fight them?" asked Freeblade.

"No. Hungry men will hunt a deer," Lionheart said. "Even if they are searching for something else."

"Well done," murmured Freeblade. "I'm glad no fight was necessary. The less attention drawn to us, the better."

Lionheart smiled. "Did you think they might take notice of bears and stags and wolves fighting side-by-side?"

His smile went away. "But it was not without price," he added. "I have a stag with an arrow through his shoulder. I must tend to him as well." He wheeled the lion about and they were gone.

The soldier at their feet groaned and stirred.

"Stay here on guard, Freeblade, if you wish," said Wordsmith. "I will tend to this one's wounds, since he still lives. We owe him that, at least."

Freeblade agreed. "Let us be kind to our enemies, even though we half-slay them first."

Wordsmith worked his arms beneath the fallen man's form, lifted and shouldered him awkwardly away. His limp, never entirely absent, was exaggerated by the cumbersome weight.

Groping in the shadows, Freeblade recovered the fallen weapons and considered them with his fingers. He stacked the bow and arrows against a tree as useless in the dark, but tucked the soldier's sword into his belt.

He resumed his watch, seeing little enough with his eyes but trusting his ears more.

Lionheart found him there later, still standing motionless in the forest like a patient tree.

"Come," he said to Freeblade. "That danger is gone now. The animals will tell us if the soldiers return."

* * *

The soldier woke to pulsing pain and found himself on a pallet of rushes, the sounds of life playing around him.

He groaned and tried with little success to move his limbs. His head ached violently, his right hand was heavily bandaged, his left hand was fastened to the window framing with a long leather strap, and one leg was splinted with rough lengths of wood and layers of wrapped cloth.

He looked up at the man standing by the pallet and understood at once who had defeated him.

"You are Freeblade," he stated weakly, but without hesitation. "I fought you in the arena, and I would not have willingly fought you again."

"And you are Arden," Freeblade replied. "I remember you well from the tournament."

Arden raised his right arm a few excruciating inches. "What have you done to me?" he asked dully.

"Your fingers are gone," answered Freeblade calmly, "and your leg is broken. Your head is apparently too hard to be damaged, for even though I knocked you senseless you woke again quickly. Your fever is rising."

"Why did you not kill me?" he asked.

"I have no taste for death," answered Freeblade, turning his head away. "I have already seen too much of it," he continued softly. "When I must use force, I will. But if I may fulfill my mission without taking life, I shall."

"There will be slaughter soon enough," Arden said.

"Was that your mission? To find and slaughter us?"

Arden said nothing, and Freeblade was not sure he would answer at all. "It was a mission of shame," he finally admitted, "and one I had no taste for.

"We came to kill a child."

Freeblade's blood slowed in his veins and chilled his heart.

"A child?" he prompted, his voice concealing his anxiety.

"Fame has heard rumors of a child," Arden explained, pain striping his voice and features with darkness. "A child who will take his throne from him.

"For months now no child has been born in Glory, and there are no children waiting to be born—a bane of barrenness he blames on the beggar and those of you who followed him. It had to be Covenant's doing, for wasn't one of his company with child? What other child could it be?

" 'Find her,' Fame said, 'and kill her and her child.' "

Then they do not yet know about the Child, thought Freeblade. "And you came here, searching?" he probed.

Arden shook his head. "We had been searching to the south and were on our way back to Glory empty-handed. I lost the others on our short cut to the road."

Then our secret is still safe, thought Freeblade. *But this one cannot be allowed to leave us. What can we do with him?*

The Child entered, unbidden; the fallen soldier could not take his eyes from him.

Freeblade moved to place himself between Arden and the Child, but the Child prevented him with a bare shake of his head.

"Who is this?" Arden demanded in a hoarse whisper.

"This is the Child," Freeblade said, a warning rumbling beneath the surface of his voice. "The Everlasting Child."

"I know now," whispered the soldier after a few long moments of silence and contemplation. "The child we seek is not one yet to be born. It is *this* one."

"All seek this Child, whether they know it or not," said Freeblade.

A somber but not unfriendly expression on his face, the Child reached forward and laid his hands on Arden's chest. Then the fever boiled in the soldier's head, and he drifted back to sleep.

* * *

The Child slumbered on Beauty's shoulder as Freeblade talked with her and Wordsmith.

"What can we do with him?" Freeblade asked. "If he leaves here with knowledge of us, the soldiers will return."

"But can you kill him in cold blood?" Beauty asked.

"No," Freeblade admitted, "only when the blood pumps hot would I strike a mortal blow."

"And this is no longer combat," Beauty pointed out.

"Yet it may still be war," Freeblade returned.

The Child woke from his nap. Beauty lowered him to the ground and asked him plaintively, "What would you have us do with Arden?"

But the Child only smiled at them and wandered off to play.

"I think he has given us his answer," murmured Beauty. "And the answer may be that no answer is needful yet."

"His calm is contagious, isn't it?" remarked Wordsmith.

*　*　*

Arden still slept, oppressed by fever, when Freeblade came to change his bandages. Freeblade unwrapped the last layer around Arden's hand and stopped suddenly, frozen by what he saw. Hurrying off, he returned shortly with Wordsmith and Beauty behind him.

"Look at this!" he exclaimed.

The stumps of Arden's fingers had healed over cleanly. There was no blood, no oozing, no need for a bandage.

They quickly unwrapped his leg, and Beauty pronounced the break healed, as far as she could tell from the outside. There was no ugly swelling, no bruised and puffy flesh, no angle where the broken bones had been imperfectly aligned.

They looked at each other.

"The Child?" suggested Wordsmith.

"Who else?" answered Beauty. "Is anyone else here a source of miracles?"

"Yet he still has a fever," replied Freeblade, looking at the soldier, "and he tosses and moans in his sleep. Is that healing?"

Beauty shrugged. "Leave him be," she said, "and watch him. Perhaps the fever is part of the miracle."

Freeblade found Lionheart and arranged a guard of wolves for Arden. Then he dragged himself wearily to his own pallet in search of long-denied rest.

This healing is like Covenant among us again, he thought as he lay down. *Except that the fingers were not restored, merely healed over. Is that the price of being an enemy? But if Arden is an enemy, why heal him at all?*

Sleep finally overcame his puzzlement.

* * *

Not until after the next morning's meal did Freeblade hear any stirring from Arden. He greeted the wolves with a caress, slipped inside the house and found the fever broken and the soldier lying quietly on the pallet.

Arden's eyes turned toward Freeblade and locked their gazes together. Arden raised his healed hand, not so much in welcome as in display. "This is no ordinary child," he said, "to have this kind of power."

"It was the Child's doing," admitted Freeblade. "He healed your leg as well."

"And my head too." Arden let his outstretched arm fall back onto the blanket. "Tell me more of him," he implored. "He has haunted my dreams, and I have thought of little save him."

Freeblade hesitated. *How much should he know?*

"What is his name?" Arden began.

"To us he is simply the Child."

"Does he speak at all?" the soldier asked.

Freeblade shook his head.

"He said no word in my dreams, either," continued Arden. "He said nothing at all, but again and again he beckoned me to stand beside you and follow him. He beckoned, and I obeyed, and I knelt to him. I would do so now in person, for this Child is irresistible, and has claimed my trust and my service." He hesitated then, and finally continued, "But I must know if I can trust *you.*"

"If I had wished you dead," responded Freeblade, "I would have slain you on the road. How do I know that *I* can trust *you?*"

Arden nodded. "A fair question. I swore fealty to Fame when I beheld his power. I swore fealty to the Child when I beheld his love."

"Was it feigned?"

"Neither to Fame nor to the Child. I gave the best I had, to the best I could find."

"But will your loyalty change again when something greater overwhelms you?"

"I do not know," Arden confessed. "When I beheld Fame's power, I could imagine nothing greater. When the Child's love came to me, the lure of power faded. Is there any force greater than love, that the memory of the Child would pale beside it?"

"We have found nothing like it."

"Then I am as loyal as you are. I have bent my knee to greatness wherever I have encountered it."

"It is one thing to kneel," Freeblade said, "and quite another to fight. How will you fight at all? Your hand is useless for the sword."

"Yes, but I still have another hand." He grinned and beckoned for his sword with his left hand.

Freeblade looked at the extra sword in his belt and hesitated. "I cannot make such a decision on my own. I must first speak with Wordsmith."

Before Freeblade could rise, the door opened and the Child walked in.

Arden struggled from the pallet and knelt awkwardly on the floor, offering a stuttered oath of loyalty. This time Freeblade made no move to interfere.

Moving calmly and purposefully, the Child drew the sword from Freeblade's belt, carried it to Arden and left it with him. Arden called his surprised thanks after him, and the Child turned in the doorway and beamed his smile on both of them, a smile that warmed the air long after the giver was gone.

Arden eyed Freeblade. "You wished to see the one called Wordsmith?"

"No," answered Freeblade eventually, "I don't think that will be necessary. The trust of the Child has been laid on you."

"Then I would accept the challenge as well."

Arden balanced his sword in his good hand and cut a delicate pattern of swirls in the air. "The old warrior who taught me insisted that I learn to use both hands equally well. Besides, I have enough hand left for this." His right hand a mere blur in the shadows, he drew a knife from behind his belt and brandished it, the leather strap still fitting snugly around his thumb and over his palm.

Freeblade felt suddenly cold, realizing he had missed the man's small weapon every time they had ministered to him. "You could have used that anytime already," he said hollowly.

"So I could have, but I didn't. You defeated me in fair combat, and I know an honorable man when I meet one."

"Arden," said Freeblade gravely, "you stood against me not once but twice, first as an opponent and then as an enemy. Now you must either stand with me or stand out of my way. I am committed to the Child, in life and in death. If you share that burden and are willing to wear those same chains, then you may stand beside me."

Arden nodded, concealing the knife again in his belt, and Freeblade helped him to his feet.

"I am whole again," he said, "but I am still stiff."

"Perhaps the echo of the miracle was left as a reminder of the miracle," Freeblade suggested. "It seems that we are always to be amazed and reminded of the unimaginable things that have been done for us."

* * *

That evening Freeblade faced the rest of the Company around the fire. "Arden has chosen to join us," he began, "to protect us as he once sought to destroy us."

None seemed surprised, though a few were hesitant to hear the soldier's wishes so boldly stated. Freeblade's own acceptance surprised him, but then ever since the beggar he had surprised himself many times.

"I would have my own doubts," explained Freeblade, "but the Child has accepted him—healed him, given him back his sword and shown his trust. How can I override that approval, even if I wished?"

"The Child speaks for us all," said Wordsmith, "even though he utters no words. Welcome to the Company of Covenant, Arden."

Arden expressed his quiet thanks.

"We have a custom in this Company," continued Wordsmith, "begun by Covenant himself. Save one, all of us bear a new name that was given us when he changed our lives.

"You know our names now, but you do not know our former names, nor the stories behind them."

Brightface told her story, and then Binder, and after that Wordsmith turned to Arden again.

"It is fitting, I believe, that you should leave the name of Arden in the dust, as I did once, and be known by a better one."

Arden thought. "I would take a name that embraces my future without denying my past—yet a name that sets forth what I must do now."

"Halfhand?" suggested Binder, only partly serious.

Arden paused, then nodded. "That would do nicely," he said.

Surprise showed on Freeblade's face. "That is hardly a noble name."

"But it is the mark of my humiliation, is it not?" asked Arden. "The defeat that brought me low and into the hands of the Child? I would gladly give my other hand if need be to claim that privilege. Let me be Halfhand, then, if that seems a good thing to you."

Wordsmith gestured to Freeblade. "I leave that decision to you, Freeblade. You conquered him, and then spared his life; he is your right arm now, though he does not have all his own."

"I cannot make that decision," said Freeblade. "He who names a thing has power over it. So it is with a king and his subjects, with parents and their children, and even children with their kittens. I am not comfortable with that kind of power over this man."

"But I am content with that," Arden insisted. "So it shall be with this warrior and his leader. I bow to you, and accept the name you give me."

"I am not your leader," said Freeblade. "I follow the Child."

"Then I will follow where you go," said Arden simply, and only Wordsmith could add to his words.

"Then let us consider Arden slain in the heat of battle," he pronounced. "Welcome, Halfhand."

Freeblade rose and offered his hand. "Come," he said, "let us fight, not as foes now, but as men do who sharpen one another even with dull edges. I have power, and you have skill. Let us spar, with stick and padded blade, and learn from one another, and practice for the day we hope never comes."

Wordsmith watched them go. "Covenant said we would destroy all our enemies," he said quietly to Beauty, "one way or another. I like this way the best."

TWELVE

Toward
the
Sea

THE MORNING HAD BARELY BEGUN WHEN THE CHILD BROUGHT
Freeblade to Wordsmith and Beauty and then sat to draw in
the soft, bare earth. With only a few strokes of a stick in the
sand, he sketched a scene that leaped full-grown from their
memories.

"This is Graycove!" exclaimed Freeblade.

"And the island," said Wordsmith.

"And the *Childsbreath*," added Beauty.

The Child moved his stick again and added three figures to
the *Childsbreath* and one to the island. Finally, he drew three
large figures and one small one at the edge of Graycove, and
pointed to himself, Wordsmith, Beauty and Freeblade.

"We are to go?" Freeblade asked, knowing his words were
not truly needed.

The Child nodded.

"Shall we ride the lions?" Beauty asked Wordsmith.

The Child shook his head, smiling.

Beauty knelt to him. "Are we walking the whole way?"

The Child nodded.

Freeblade shrugged. "Graycove is many miles from here," he said, "but we have walked greater distances before."

* * *

"The Child has called us to return to Graycove," Wordsmith told the rest of the Company late that afternoon. "He and Freeblade and Beauty and I will leave as soon as the morning sun lights our path.

"Binder, Brightface, Lionheart—I leave you in charge again." He turned to Halfhand. "I would ask of you a harder job," said Freeblade. "Mine is the sword that is bound to defend the Child, but you are a free champion. Stay in Heartshope and guard its people. And listen to Lionheart, for he listens to the watchers who are everywhere and who need less sleep than we do."

"It is good that we have two swords," nodded Wordsmith, "for once again the Company must walk two separate paths."

* * *

Beauty glanced at Wordsmith's eyes in the raw bright morning light and knew he had spent a restless night.

"Dreams?" she murmured.

"Dreams," he nodded, rubbing his eyes where the sleepless hours had left them raw and stinging. "Or visions, or whatever you choose to call them." He waved his hand toward the fire outside. "I do not think we shall meet here again."

"What does that mean? Another prophecy understood?"

Wordsmith shook his head. "A conviction, a sense that when the Child begins this journey he will not stop until all is done. But that may be only fit, for how could all things end *here*? That is not what we have been told to expect. All roads, straight or winding, lead back to Glory at last."

"Yet we are going to the sea, not to Glory," Beauty pointed out.

"I do not plan these events," said Wordsmith. "I only sense their patterns."

* * *

There had been little to prepare, and now they were ready to go.

The Child stretched out his arms to Beauty, and she gladly picked him up. His soft arms closed around her neck, but then she felt his fingers tugging at the clasp of her necklace, from which dangled the mirror piece.

She drew back her head just as the Child lifted her necklace away. Then he turned his eyes to Brightface and beckoned to her. She came to him, and he draped the necklace about her neck.

"I guess you are to have it now," Beauty said.

"I will wear it if you wish," she said. "But why should I have it?"

Beauty shook her head. "It is not mine to keep or bestow. It was Covenant's mirror long before I saw it, and I gladly yield the Child power to pass it to you."

"What shall I do with it?" Brightface asked.

The Child turned back to Beauty and contentedly buried his face in her shoulder.

She shifted his weight to that side and said, "I don't know."

"We know Covenant's ways," said Wordsmith, "and we are beginning to know the Child's. Take the mirror, and when the need comes I am sure you will understand the gift."

She looked into its depths. "It is dark," she said flatly.

"Covenant made this," Beauty reminded her, "and it has his magic in it. It cannot stay dark forever."

* * *

In Beauty's arms the Child bid Heartshope farewell. *His hugs had been warm and happy, but his eyes suddenly are so sad,* thought Beauty. *Does he expect to see this place again?*

The first steps of their journey carried them past the ruined graveyard of the lepers. Wordsmith wondered again at the mysteries there, but despite all their shared questions and speculations, they had no firm idea why some small share of the graves had been shaken open and now gaped empty.

After the first few miles, the Child indicated that he wished to walk. Wordsmith, whose shoulders had taken over from Beauty's arms, was grateful. Even so, the Child himself grew tired in another few miles, but would not cease walking.

"Do we stop here?" asked Freeblade.

The Child shook his head and stumbled on.

Freeblade stooped to pick him up, but Wordsmith prevented him.

"Let me," said Wordsmith. "You should have your arms free for your sword. I cannot guard us."

"Cannot your songs defend us?"

"Perhaps to drive our enemies away," he smiled in answer. Then he began singing, and his voice lightened their weariness. And with the Child to hold and behold and walk beside, the miles passed almost unnoticed under their feet.

*   *   *

"We have visitors," Lionheart told Binder and Halfhand. "A dozen people have turned from the road to Glory and are coming this way."

"Soldiers?" asked Binder at once.

"No," replied Lionheart. "Men and women both, and perhaps a child or two. My friends have left them alone, for I thought it best if we three met them on the way."

"We shall, then," stated Halfhand, tightening his sword belt. His actions drew Brightface to them, and she heard the news from Binder.

"Let me go too," she said.

Binder caught Halfhand's eye, and they pondered silently.

"We do not know who these people are," said Binder. "They may be our friends, they may be our enemies, or they may be only travelers."

"We may still have friends in Glory," said Brightface. "Many people came to the daily feast. I may know some of them if I see their faces."

"You may watch us from the shelter of the trees," Binder consented. "If they do fall upon us, then you can return to rouse the rest."

"Lionheart," said Halfhand, "send your beasts to watch all around Heartshope. If I were attacking this place, I would create just such a diversion so I could approach from behind."

Lionheart nodded. "I will come to you later." He disappeared, moving like the animals he had come to lead.

*   *   *

"I wonder why we are not riding," said Beauty the next afternoon, washing her tired feet in a brook.

"I do not know," replied Wordsmith, bathing his own feet and the Child's while watching Freeblade prowl the edges of the clearing where they rested. "Perhaps Lionheart and the animals have other duties to attend, if not now, then soon."

The Child smiled his thanks at Wordsmith as they moved on, his usual silence saying more than only words could.

From time to time Wordsmith sang, but softly, and only in places where they could see well around them, or where his voice would not carry far. Heartshope had held them safe for so long. Now they traveled almost alone in a landscape that sometimes seemed strange.

*   *   *

Halfhand and Binder stood on the dusty path and faced the travelers. They recognized none as faces that had once sat at Covenant's table.

"We would see the Child," one of them said simply.

"Tell me of this Child," responded Halfhand. "Who is he?"

"He is Covenant come again," said one woman firmly.

"He is the child of many rumors," answered a man.

"Why do you seek such a one here?" asked Halfhand. "This

is a place of wild animals, where disease has held sway for many years. We who live here only wish to be left in peace."

"Nevertheless, we would see him."

"There is no Child here," said Binder, unsure if his accurate words could be counted as truth. *Why am I uneasy?* he thought. *They have not come with weapons drawn, but I still smell the presence of an enemy.*

Behind him, distrust pounded in Brightface's mind as well. *Why did the Child and the others have to leave?* she thought. *He could have showed us, and Wordsmith, Beauty or Freeblade would at least give guidance. I wish I could call them back for this decision.*

The mirror fragment grew hot against her skin. She pulled it from her cloak and gingerly turned it over in her fingers. It flashed in her grasp and gave her sudden hope.

The mirror, she thought. *Maybe the Child has already provided help!*

Without waiting for new fears to overwhelm her, she stepped boldly out of the cover of trees and walked forward to take her place beside Binder.

Binder saw her, frowned and beckoned Halfhand to withdraw with him for a moment. They met Brightface partway to the trees, and Lionheart appeared then to join them.

"I am afraid," whispered Binder. "These may not all be our friends."

"But how can we tell?" asked Halfhand. "Remember, I was once an enemy."

"But the Child accepted you," said Brightface.

"And the Child is not here to deal with these."

Binder turned to Lionheart. "Do the animals know? Can they tell who means to harm us?"

Lionheart listened to words the others could not hear. "No," he said at last, "but they are troubled too, for some they do not trust. Something is not right here."

"But something else *is* right," said Brightface, looking down and holding out the glass on its chain. "The mirror is bright!" she said wonderingly.

"What does it show you?" asked Lionheart.

She gazed into the shiny depths. "It is not me," she answered softly. "But I would like to be like this someday."

Binder looked over her shoulder, and they both saw a white-clad shining lady. Behind her was a radiant man. Both looked familiar but far too pure to be real.

"It is you," Binder breathed, "and me as well. Not as we are, but as we shall be. The mirror is working again."

Brightface nodded. "But what does it mean now?"

"I think," said Lionheart, "that you should ask each traveler here to look over your shoulder."

She gazed at Lionheart for a long moment, trying to guess his meaning.

"Yes," she said abruptly. "This is a good thing you have said."

They returned to the travelers. Brightface held the mirror for each and gazed at their reflected faces, trying to keep any expression from her own. Most reflections matched her radiance, but four repelled her because of their darkness.

They were puzzled by her actions. Some looked unhappy, and all wondered when Brightface asked four of them to go with Halfhand. "This is a hard thing, Lionheart," Brightface murmured as they stepped away.

"Yes," agreed Lionheart, "but swords are not the only sharp things that are a terror to the terrible." He followed Halfhand and the four away from the path, over the rise of the hill and deeper into the stand of trees.

A trio of bears lumbered after him.

Brightface led the rest down the path to Heartshope, where arms spread wide to welcome them.

*　*　*

Twisting his fingers into theirs, the Child walked happily between Beauty and Wordsmith.

"Do you think they will be all right without us?" asked Wordsmith. "No leaders are indispensable, but we are the three who have taken the most responsibility. We *are* far from Heartshope and moving farther away with every step."

"Look at the Child," answered Beauty. "Does he seem worried?"

* * *

"And the others?" Brightface inquired of Halfhand and Lionheart later.

"They are not here," answered Halfhand. "We guarded them as far as the road and pointed them back to Glory."

"Was that enough to protect us?" she asked. "They must realize that we are the ones they seek, whether or not the Child is here."

"I was still uneasy, but unwilling to do more," Halfhand said. "They walked off, but as they left I glimpsed the bears in the distance."

Lionheart took up the thread of the conversation. "The bears distrusted them, and I fear they followed in pursuit. As to what the bears did, I cannot say."

"But there was to be no more hunting, no more killing here in Wildhaven!" she protested.

"We stood on its border as we parted," Binder pointed out.

"When the bears returned, they avoided me," said Lionheart, "and I could draw nothing from them. Remember that I do not control the animals, though I lead them. Perhaps they know better than I what should be done, for they have spent a lifetime judging enemies and acting to protect themselves and their kind.

"And do not forget that they have as much claim to the Child as we do, and as much right to protect him."

"Then let the fate of the wicked be upon them," Halfhand said. "I did not know what else to do, after they had failed the test of the mirror."

No one answered him, and at last he broke his own silence. "Yet another thing disturbs me," he said. "I came as an enemy, and you treated me kindly."

"Once you had been rendered powerless, anyway," added Binder.

"And you came as an open enemy," said Brightface. "You brought us danger but not deceit."

Binder nodded. "Freeblade is a man of wisdom, and he told me before he left, speaking of you, that he would rather trust a man of misplaced loyalty than a man with no loyalty at all."

THIRTEEN

The
Final
Island

THE AIR FRESHENED OVER THE HEADS OF THE CHILD AND HIS
three friends. Then one afternoon they could taste the tang
of the sea, though they could not yet see the roll of the waters.

With that scent the Child seemed restless, plucking at
Wordsmith's sleeve when they paused for rests and running
ahead a few steps to urge them on.

"This is the first time I have seen him in such a hurry,"
murmured Freeblade to Beauty.

"Great things may wait in the near distance," said Wordsmith. "Covenant's words have made straight the way for
happenings we can scarcely imagine. The Child is in the middle of them all. Perhaps he cannot wait to begin."

When they crested the last hill before Graycove, a watching
Deedtester spotted them, as though he had sensed them in the

distance. Needing no introduction to the small traveler in their midst, he came running, passing by the others to kneel before the Child. Eye to eye, they gazed into each other's face, a gaze that had been shared before but only through the veil of dreams.

"You've come at last," Deedtester breathed.

"He does not speak," cautioned Beauty.

"He doesn't have to," he replied.

The Child stretched forth his hands to brace Deedtester's cheeks; he imparted a wordless blessing that warmed the hearts of even those who merely looked on.

Deedtester opened wide his arms in supplication and offering, and the Child came to lay his head gently on the old fisherman's rough but welcoming shoulder. Deedtester wrapped his arms around the small body and stood, raising him high for all to see afresh.

"We will not need to carry him the rest of the way," whispered Wordsmith to Beauty.

"I would have to be strong indeed to pry the Child out of his arms," she whispered back. "Though newly met, they are old friends already."

"Where is Covenant?" Deedtester asked them suddenly. No one was prepared to tell the story smoothly, but after they reached Deedtester's cottage and greeted Joykeeper and Seaswallower, Wordsmith began. He related the tales of all that had happened since they had last seen Graycove, beginning with their return to Glory and ending with the Child.

"You believed," ended Wordsmith, "and now you have seen."

"I cannot believe that he is dead," said Deedtester. "Yet in some dark way I am not surprised, for wherever there is a good man evil follows after."

"I do not know for certain that he is dead," said Wordsmith, "but I can find no easy explanation besides death for his absence."

"Dark things have happened here as well," said Deedtester after a pause.

"Speak," said Wordsmith. "We have already laid our sad burdens upon you."

Deedtester related recent events for his visitors. Graycove, too, had felt the wrench of the earthquake and had seen the mystery of the abandoned graves. "And the fishing has fallen away into a mockery of a catch," he added. "The boats go out, the boats return, and there is little in the holds to tell the one from the other. Even the gulls grow scarce, and fewer crows come to pick at the discarded fish."

"We have heard of such a happening," said Beauty. "The animals everywhere are drawing away from people, except where they come to us in Heartshope. Could the fish be a part of this as well?"

"Whatever the answer, the people are muttering and saying that before long no village will be able to survive here."

The small party soon turned their talk back to the joy of their meeting again, the flow of their talk washing the rest of the day away.

"You have come. You have fulfilled the promise," said Deedtester.

"Not until we return to the island," countered Wordsmith.

"Didn't Covenant promise that he himself would return there?" asked Joykeeper.

"So I thought, at first, but now I believe that he promised *we* would return," Wordsmith responded, including Beauty and Freeblade in the sweep of his arm.

The Child, comfortable now in Joykeeper's arms, approved with a smile.

Wordsmith hesitated. "But I think we all should go. Deedtester, Joykeeper, Seaswallower."

"Have you a reason?" asked Joykeeper, puzzled.

"When the Child pictured this place for us, he drew three of you on the *Childsbreath*. Beyond that, I have only a strong feeling, born from reading this book of Covenant's promises and prophecies. As I read, and look about me with open eyes, I am more than ever convinced that when the Child came a corner was turned, and this kingdom began a headlong rush toward the fulfillment of all that Covenant said." Wordsmith tapped the book with his fingers. "These are Covenant's final words, and certain of them haunted my dreams last night. Sometimes the pressure of the promises is strongest just before the prophecy comes true."

"Whatever the Child wishes, that we will do," stated Deedtester.

"And I think that you three should also be prepared to turn your backs to Graycove," continued Wordsmith, "for I have an uneasy feeling that we might not return to this cottage. If you have anything small that you treasure, bring it with you aboard the *Childsbreath*."

They looked at him, not knowing what else to do but accept and follow.

"Then let us sleep," suggested Deedtester, "and take sail with the light and the morning tide."

* * *

The seven searchers lined the rail of the *Childsbreath*, rocking gently with the ocean swells and scanning the sea for the island.

When they saw it, Wordsmith said flatly, "This cannot be the same island."

"It is in the same place, but the shore is not the same shape," said Freeblade, "and the building has changed."

"Changed? It is all gone now!" exclaimed Wordsmith.

At first, Beauty did not recognize the island either. All the great rambling half-ruined buildings had been pulled down. A new finger of stone stretched out from the shore, and a few scattered birds of the sea waded and browsed among the tumbled rocks there.

"Not all of it," said Beauty. "Look there, beneath the trees."

Wreathed in shade that was too bright to be shadow, only a single white stone structure stood on the island.

The keel of the *Childsbreath* ground gently into the sand, and Freeblade splashed into the shallows and turned to help the rest. To their surprise the Child sat placidly along the bow of the boat and waved them on with his hand.

Shrugging his shoulders, Freeblade helped Beauty and Wordsmith over the side, and they waded across the wet sand. As they climbed the path from the sea, they passed the multitude of stones that had been tumbled into the restless waters.

And there the hermit came to meet them.

His eyes were clear and bright, his head was high, and all the shadows of haunting and hollowness had fallen away.

"Can you be Grimshade?" Beauty cried to the man, surprised.

"I remember that name," he said, "though it was lifted from my shoulders by the beggar who was more than he seemed." He smiled. "Now I am only a nameless man on a' nameless island."

"What has happened here?" asked Wordsmith. "Share your good news with us!"

"Gladly," said the hermit, ushering them farther up the path. "I have found the treasure Covenant set me to find." He pointed to the tiny house and waved them all inside. The white stone walls gleamed in the light that streamed through the ample, open windows. A matching white stone altar stood alone against the wall, its surface dusted but empty. Beauty could see neither dirt nor cobweb anywhere, though the inevitable sand had begun its drift over the sill again.

"This once was the house," he said, "so long ago I scarcely remembered it, or recognized it.

"The old ghosts have died, as you know," he began, "and they have stayed dead. Now the old fears that fed them are gone, and so are the old rotting rooms that housed them. The very stones have been cast into the sea, for I have no need to hide—now or ever again."

"Did you undo all this yourself?" asked Beauty.

"I began the work. I tore down whatever I could and cast it into the sea. But some walls remained, until I was aided by a mighty earthquake. Stone fell, the earth rippled, and waves pounded the sand without mercy."

Freeblade glanced at Wordsmith. "We have heard of that quake. Indeed, we felt it in Glory."

Grimshade looked at them. "Could not Covenant be with you?" he asked. "I wanted him to see this island."

This time Freeblade gave the explanation, and Grimshade took it with sadness, joy and bewilderment.

"I think," offered Wordsmith, "that Covenant knew quite well what this island looked like in the past and would look like again before you even began to clean it."

"His ways were like that," added Beauty. "Whenever we would believe we had discovered something new, we would realize that we were finding nothing more than his old hand-iwork."

Then they heard voices behind them and were joined by the Child, Deedtester and Joykeeper. Seaswallower still stood on the deck, but he could see them clearly.

Beauty made introductions. "And this is the Child," she concluded, "who walks in Covenant's ways." The hermit listened spellbound to the story of the search upon the mountain and could scarcely take his eyes from the face of the Child.

When Beauty had finished, the hermit stood, and with a wave of his hand invited the Child into the house. The Child took his hand and left dancing footprints beside the long, straight marks of the older man. They spent much time in silence inside, and there was no way to tell what passed between them. While exploring the island, Beauty glanced through one window; she could see the Child sitting upon the altar as though he belonged there and the man who had once been Grimshade kneeling on the floor.

FOURTEEN

Fire
and
Water

YOU NEED A NAME," WORDSMITH SAID TO THE HERMIT LATER.

"Covenant promised me one," came the reply, "but he told me nothing of what he had in mind."

"He said nothing to me, either," said Wordsmith, "but I would choose a name that would have pleased him. Let us call the others and see what they have to say."

But neither Beauty nor the fishing family knew what Covenant might have intended. Beauty asked the Child to help them, but received only his smile and momentarily lingering embrace.

In the distance they could see the string of fishing boats returning to Graycove. No bright flags flew from their masts, indicating no great catch in their holds.

"Empty again," said Deedtester. "This coast is slowly dying."

He turned to the hermit. "Are you not perishing as well? Do the fish still fall to your net and line?"

"I have gone hungry often," said the hermit, "but I must stay. First Covenant gave me my life again, then he gave me a task."

"You have fulfilled that task. You found the treasure of the first room and the waiting altar."

The hermit shook his head. "There is more. He called me his final man in the west and said that I would have the first sight of the final fires."

"Do you know what he meant?" asked Beauty.

"I do not," he answered, "but I am not sure that duty requires a clear understanding."

"I have a name in mind for you now," offered Beauty.

"I do, as well," said Wordsmith.

"I yield to you," she said.

"And I to you," he returned.

"Westerkeep," they said together and fell silent with surprise.

"An inspired name, obviously," observed Freeblade, "and a fitting one, since he is the man who has kept the west for Covenant."

Wordsmith saw the dignity of the name seep into the hermit's face. "So be it," he said. "Westerkeep, we are honored to be on your island."

Westerkeep welcomed them over again, and they fell to watching the Child enjoying the beach. He was in no apparent hurry to leave, playing in the mist from the waves along the sand and ignoring, for now, the *Childsbreath*.

His hands were delicate and wonderful, and they fascinated Westerkeep anew as they nimbly fingered the wet sand and built forms that had never taken shape before. He brought them into existence, and with the next surging wave up the shoreline they were gone.

"He is not making copies," Westerkeep said in hushed tones.

"He is making things never known before."

"Yes," nodded Beauty, no longer surprised but still much amazed. "These are things only he has seen."

"And now what?" asked Westerkeep, changing the subject.

"It looks as though we are meant to sleep on the island tonight," replied Wordsmith.

"I would rather sleep on the *Childsbreath*," said Deedtester.

"And I, too," added Joykeeper, "not because I love the water, but because Deedtester will be there."

"It matters not," said Westerkeep, waving his arm at the open sand. "The boat waits patiently, a bed that rocks with no hand to sway it, and this soft sand yields room for everyone, anywhere."

* * *

"We have come again to the end of the world," said Wordsmith, walking the length of the sand with Beauty before they slept. "Nothing out there exists but the water that never ends."

Beauty shivered delicately. "The end of the world. I can think of two meanings for that single phrase."

He swung her to him and tightened his arms around her waist. "I meant only that there is no land beyond this point."

She settled her cheek on his chest and murmured, "You have studied Covenant's words for so long that sometimes you sound like him—and leave me looking for double meanings in everything."

"I love you," said Wordsmith softly. "How many meanings can you find in that?"

She smiled. "Give me time to count them."

* * *

Westerkeep shook Freeblade and Wordsmith awake in the night, and Beauty in the process as well. "Come quickly," he said. "You must see this!"

Freeblade thought first of the Child, but saw him asleep in Beauty's arms.

"What is it?" he whispered back.

"I am not sure," Westerkeep answered, "but Covenant told me I would see it."

Freeblade stumbled outside into the dark and followed him to the peak of the island. Beauty, still bearing the sleeping Child, came next, with Wordsmith just behind her.

From the other side of the hill came Seaswallower, with Deedtester and Joykeeper rubbing the sleep from their eyes.

"There," said Westerkeep, pointing directly to the west. "The sea is burning."

Vast bands of light danced on the horizon, out past the banks where fish had once sported, where giant flames now began to bloom and lick the surface of the water.

"Can this be fire?" asked Freeblade.

"Covenant said I would see the ocean burn," said Joykeeper. "What else could it be?"

"When did this start?" asked Wordsmith.

"Not long ago," said Westerkeep. "I made sure of what I was seeing, then came for you straight away."

The Child stirred in Beauty's arms, and she gazed down at his face. His eyes, enormous in the dark, reflected the ribbon of the far-off flames. Again she saw wonder there, though a wonder unmixed with surprise. His heart pounded, and his fingers clung to her cloak with new energy. In another boy she might have called it fear, but in the Child she could only believe it anticipation.

Their own emotions ranged from awe to bewilderment. Each one had formed some vague idea of the "final fires," but none had imagined anything like this.

"What do we do now?" asked Freeblade.

"Let us sit and watch," said Wordsmith. "I would see what happens next."

* * *

The morning light could not dispel the brightness of the flames, nor could it hide the fact that the fires grew closer with every passing moment.

"This is no ordinary fire," observed Beauty. "But then, what *has* been ordinary for us?"

" 'The fire that burns at the heart of the earth,' " recited Wordsmith. "Now it burns upon the surface."

"Covenant said that I would see this ocean burn," Joykeeper said again. "He called it my 'old enemy,' and so it has been."

"Now it rises against you in a new and different way."

"It is time to leave this island behind," said Westerkeep. "The flames come, and we have seen them. We should not wait for them here."

Freeblade's gaze asked the question for all of them.

"I am afraid," Westerkeep explained.

"Of this island?" asked Beauty.

"Not of this island, but of what may become of it. When the earthquake struck the island and wild waves hammered at the sand, the earth shivered, the land dropped lower in the waters, and the surf surged farther up the shore.

"I have heard that islands rise and islands sink with the restless heaving of the earth, and though this place is a wonder it is a fragile one.

"I fear another earthquake or some other disaster. Have you noticed?" he asked, sweeping his arm about them. "Every bird that can fly has taken to the air again, just as they did the last time the earth shook itself."

"And the sea is far too quiet for me," added Deedtester. "He may indeed be right."

In only moments they had retrieved their packs and waded out to the waiting *Childsbreath*. They had barely wrestled the anchor aboard when an eerie calm fell heavily around them.

"It begins," said Wordsmith quietly.

"The beginning of the end," added Beauty, thinking of Wordsmith's words the night before, but watching the Child's face as she swept him into her arms.

The island began to tremble, and the sea shuddered violently beneath them, though they could not feel the movement in the boat. Trees danced on the island and waved their fronds gracefully in the unnaturally still air.

The earthquake was not violent, but it shook their hearts with its firm thunder, rumbling for a short eternity before ceasing abruptly.

"There will be waves to deal with, and the highest will come from the open sea," said Deedtester anxiously. "Let us stay in the lee of this island until the worst is past."

They all scanned the trembling sea between the *Childsbreath* and the distant land.

Little ripples ringed the ocean, as though the waves could no longer decide which way to run.

Then the seas began to lift in the west, blotting out the bottom half of the distant flames. Deedtester headed the *Childsbreath* into the growing swells.

*   *   *

The people of Graycove had seen the strange lights dancing in the night on the sea. They did not know what it was, and they were deeply afraid. Some thought it was the sun again, halted on its course and sent backward over the world from the west.

But the real dawn bloomed pale in the east, and they searched for other explanations. No boats stirred, and no one sailed forth to see the lights firsthand.

Then the earthquake leveled all that had not been firmly built, and the following waves pounded deep over the sand and destroyed more of the village.

When the *Childsbreath* glided into the harbor, the panic sparked by flames and quakes and waves had been rekindled by a new terror.

The graveyard above the town had ripped apart, and the bodies buried there had risen to roam the village. The amazement and terror they caused was unbounded, for many of those who had come back from the dead were remembered

well—evil at worst and indifferent at best. They still bore the marks of their deaths; wounds gaped bloodlessly, broken limbs dangled uselessly, and disease-shriveled chests hung empty and airless even as they walked about.

Yet they harmed no one, said nothing and wandered vacantly through the ruins of the village.

Then, all along the shore, the sea also began to give up her dead. The violent but diminishing waves threw corpses ashore, pale and weakly silent, that eventually stirred themselves and began to walk again.

All the graves were burst open now, though not all of the missing had emerged from the waves. Some pondered in their panic why the best men of memory all remained shrouded in the moldy hold of the earth and the blue-black vaults of the sea.

Hovering safely off the ruins of the pier, the crew of the *Childsbreath* could see all things plainly.

"Why have some returned from the dead and some not?" asked Freeblade.

"There are no more dead," said Wordsmith. "All the graves are empty now, and all the dead are risen."

"But where are the rest of them?"

Wordsmith answered him, "Covenant said that we would see the troubled dead, but that we would have to wait to see the grateful dead."

"What did he mean?"

Wordsmith shook his head. "Again, Covenant's words mean more than we can make of them unaided. But remember our flight to Heartshope and the earthquake that shattered half the tombs on our path. Perhaps they were emptied that night and these were all that were left."

Behind them the flames grew brighter and taller and closer.

"Is the wind driving the fire?" asked Beauty.

"I do not know," answered Deedtester, "but a hot breeze licks the water, and even the sails are singed." He looked at his craft with regret. "I think it is time to land and leave her behind."

Wordsmith and Freeblade reluctantly agreed, but the Child shook his head firmly and motioned them to stay where they were.

Wordsmith looked at the rest. "His ways are hard to follow," he said, "but his judgments have never failed us. I will stay, though we burn. The rest of you may flee if you wish."

Though reluctance and fear swelled in their hearts, the rest stayed as well.

The Child pointed to the people along the shore and beckoned Wordsmith to bring them aboard as well.

* * *

The advancing flames and the *Childsbreath* did not go long unnoticed in the chaos and panic on the shore.

"To your boats," called Wordsmith across the battered sand. "Come with us or follow!"

"But all the sea is burning!" someone answered. "We have nowhere safe but the land!"

"Not even this beloved haven will endure what is to come," answered Wordsmith.

"Abandon your boat!" cried one man. "How can she save you from the flames? Flee to the hills while there is still time!"

Wherever water was the horizon, the horizon was burning.

Freeblade struggled up the mast of the *Childsbreath*. From the top he could not see over the flames, but looking inland he could see what the others could not: the surging strand of a new river carved its way to the sea.

"The melting mountain!" he called down. "Its water is here and soon will fall into the sea!

"Fire and water," he mumbled to himself. "What will happen when they collide?"

FIFTEEN

The Last Voyage

SOON THEY KNEW.

The river burst through the final hill and tumbled down the beach with a thunderous roar, sluicing dirt and mud and sand aside in its hungry rush to return its burden to the sea. The waters finally met with great violence, and when the swirl subsided, the river beckoned them on to a safe harbor.

The Child pointed onward, and finally Freeblade understood. "We shall sail straight to Glory," he said, "safe from flames, and the first ship to see those troubled walls."

The boat swiftly but smoothly heeled herself to the Child's gesture.

Deedtester gazed overboard at the flowing water. "I do not think you need my hand at the tiller any longer," he remarked.

"It is Covenant's boat," shrugged Wordsmith, "and thus the

Child's. Let him do with it what he pleases."

They passed over the turbulent, muddy meeting of the waters and began their river journey.

"If the sea is burning," asked Freeblade of no one, "how does one put it out?"

He expected no answer, but Deedtester offered one. "Perhaps it will stop at the shore, where there is no water left to burn."

Behind them the flames made the final leap to the shore, and the beached and abandoned fishing boats caught fire. Then the great trees along the shore erupted, the green wood exploding rather than burning in the fierce heat.

Graycove burned as they watched.

Those on board the *Childsbreath* could clearly see the lines of desperate people struggling up the hills, dropping their possessions as they realized the ground itself was beginning to burn.

Beauty sighed as the gap between Graycove and the *Childsbreath* widened. "They did not believe the Child would help them escape."

"Did we?" answered Wordsmith. "We clung to him, not for the sense of his words, but because we know him. Would we have followed his words alone?"

"Wordsmith," called Deedtester quietly.

"Yes?"

Deedtester pointed down at the river surging past the sides of the *Childsbreath*.

"How does she sail upstream?" he asked. "And against the wind?"

"She is the *Childsbreath*," answered Wordsmith. "Perhaps the Child breathes on her."

Deedtester gazed back at Graycove. "Even if they still had their boats," he said, "they could not readily follow. They would find it slow work alone, sailing against the current."

There was little else to say. The *Childsbreath* sailed alone and unhindered up the icy river—beyond sight of the flames, of the sea, and of any other beings save a few birds and the sun in the unblinking sky.

* * *

Lionheart woke from his doze suddenly, stirred by the clamor of a myriad of excited birds—hawks, doves, sparrows, eagles—all circling over Heartshope and calling wildly for the one man who could help them understand what they had seen.

Yet another earthquake? he thought. *I hoped the one this morning would be the last.*

He listened to them carefully and called Binder to him. "Binder," said Lionheart, "the birds bear us disturbing news. They have flown from the edges of the kingdom, from north and south and east and west. They have all seen the same horror: the land is burning. And not only the land but the sea as well. They have seen nothing like this before. The fields and forests are flaming. The mountains are burning—melting as though from great fires beneath the earth—and the hills are hidden in smoke."

"A forest fire?" asked Binder. "Everywhere at once? And how can the oceans burn?"

"If it were only one report," said Lionheart, "I would disbelieve it too. But more than a dozen birds have seen the same thing wherever the horizon lies. I believe they saw what they saw. But I don't know what it was that they saw."

The messengers continued to arrive, both birds in the air and fleet beasts on foot.

"The flames do not diminish," Lionheart reported to Binder and Halfhand later. "They are coming closer all the time, advancing as fast as one can walk unaided. Whole villages burn. The roads are filled with the fleeing. They are walking or in wagons, and they are coming this way."

"Have many died?" asked Binder.

"That is another amazing thing," replied Lionheart. "None have died, but the dead have risen and now flee with the living! Some of the living appear to have been burned, but they have all escaped ahead of the flames. The fire comes steadily, but not so swiftly that it cannot be outrun. This is disaster, but it seems that death has been set to one side."

"And the animals?" asked Binder. "Have they escaped as well?"

Lionheart regarded him solemnly.

"As for the fish in the sea, I do not know. Insects, all that creep or crawl—they must be perishing, but again I do not know for certain. We are past the season for most young; the birds and the larger beasts that remained behind have fled and are heading in our direction. Will the fires burn this far, do you think?"

Binder shook his head. "I hear the echoes of Covenant's words preserved in Wordsmith's book: 'fire, flood and famine—fear, futility and failure.' Is this what he meant?"

The question floated in the air unanswered.

* * *

With no visible hand at the tiller, the *Childsbreath* worked slowly up the new and winding river. The banks here, in what had been low desert wasteland, were already beginning to burst forth in new life that had lain dormant in the parched soil.

The Child, riding on the bow, pointed to a shallow sandbar, and the *Childsbreath* drifted to a halt beneath a pleasant stand of tall trees, old trees with new leaves and a green fuzz of vines and seedlings.

The Child went ashore and quickly fell asleep in the shade. Freeblade went with him and began exploring the riverbank.

"Freeblade," asked Wordsmith, still on the deck, "what do you see in your glass? Is it still black and blank, or can you see the distance?"

Freeblade retrieved his glass fragment from under his cloak, leaned against the peak of the mast and slowly peered in all directions.

"I see nothing but fire," he called down, "fire so bright and so widespread that little else shows."

"Look again," Wordsmith urged. "Perhaps your eyes will take time to see against the brightness."

Freeblade lifted the shiny fragment to his eye again and gazed through it for several long moments.

"The whole world is burning, but now I see people," he said finally. "People fleeing from the flames. The roads are lined with men and women on foot and clogged with their carts and wagons."

"Then the world is ending!" exclaimed Beauty.

"That is evil news to most but a sweet promise to us," said Freeblade. "Covenant said this would happen and that when it did we would have crowns! Rewards!"

"How can crowns be worth anything next to the love of the Child?" asked Beauty. "His hugs warm the heart, and his smiles give meaning to the universe."

On the bank the Child slept long and hard, as though worn by an effort no one had seen him make. After the anxiety and anticipation of the previous days, he subsided again into his previous contentment.

For the rest of that day the Child slept and played and gave and received love, and that evening he led them back on board the *Childsbreath*. She continued her breathless glide up the river.

The next day Freeblade and Beauty and Wordsmith climbed the mast and tried with the glass to read the signs of the world around them and track the progress of the relentless fires.

That afternoon Wordsmith descended with disturbing news.

"The flames are nibbling the edges of Wildhaven," he said sadly.

"And our people?" asked Freeblade.

"They have abandoned Heartshope," he said, "and are on their way to the last refuge, Glory. All the animals are with them. It is a wondrous procession."

A great sadness fell over Freeblade, and in frustration he slashed his sword in the air. "Straight into the hands of our enemies," he mourned. "Who can protect them there?"

"Has all their protection been set aside," asked Beauty, "just because they have been forced from Heartshope? Remember that we go to Glory too."

"We move too quickly," said Freeblade, "if we are to defend ourselves from Fame's wrath. Too slowly if we are to help our friends."

*   *   *

On the second day they beheld their goal in the distance.

"Glory no longer looks like Glory," said Wordsmith.

"No," agreed Beauty. The Lonely Mountain no longer rose in the background; they had expected that. But none had expected Fame's Tower to be so tall, so slim and so bright.

The spire was the first to catch the eye, gathering the first rays of the rising sun and scattering its dazzle around Glory. It was high and lifted up, a tower within a tower. On the inside a thin, tight, dizzy spiral raced for the heavens; outside and following after, a thicker spiral curled upward. Both sprouted planks and scaffolds and workers, like ants struggling up and down a high desert plant.

The inner spike seemed hardly thick enough for one man and a stair to hold him. The outer circle was wider, with a ramp broad enough to hold horses on its stairs, beasts hauling stones and mortar on their backs.

Wordsmith recalled the half-magical construction of Covenant's house and wondered if some twisted magic was at work here.

When the Mountain had towered over Glory, it had possessed a severe grandeur, but this Tower that had risen against the fall of the Mountain had an uneasy symmetry of a different kind. It seemed to grow taller as they approached—taller, but no less slender, until it seemed that image was but the fulfillment and the mark of all that Glory had been and

would ever be, as if Glory had been made for the Tower and the Tower had been made for Glory.

"No other king has so left his mark here," Freeblade remarked.

They sailed on to a landing place in the shadows of the ancient stone walls. Once a nameless rock in the valley, their anchor point was now a fine pier where the new waters swirled against the foundations. The *Childsbreath* glided forward and trembled to a halt against the sudden shore. Deedtester scrambled onto the pier, then caught a line from Seaswallower and secured it to the rocks.

The sails relaxed with a final sigh, fulfilled though no longer filled. Even the more-than-gentle breeze blowing against their faces declined to ruffle the calm fabric.

"The *Childsbreath* has come to Glory!" exclaimed Deedtester.

"And so has the Child," added Freeblade quietly.

No one came, either to greet them or to oppose them.

SIXTEEN

Glory Bound

THEY ENTERED THE UNATTENDED GATES AND FOUND THEMSELVES in a curl of chaos.

Fast riders from the corners of the kingdom continued to arrive, bearing news of the ongoing destruction and the burning borders.

The generations of the dead shambled in the streets, silent and with no clear purpose in their wanderings. They slept not, and ate nothing, but continued to search with empty eyes and hollow hearts for something no one else could imagine.

"There is no order here," said Deedtester. "Is Glory always like this?"

"No," said Wordsmith, "but Fame has more now than he can handle. This is panic, and I doubt that soldiers will be spared now to look for us—if they even know we are here."

"We have no place to stay," said Wordsmith.

"If everyone has fled to Glory," said Beauty, "then we will not be alone in the streets."

"Perhaps it is best this way," said Freeblade. "If we keep moving through the crowds, we will be hard to find."

The Child tugged at Beauty's sleeve, as though he had a destination in mind, and the seven began to pick their way through the eddying streets. Their way drew them into the shadow of the Tower, and Beauty was shocked to see the scowl on the Child's face as he looked up at the stone-lined spire.

Then he looked only sad, immensely sad—an expression that did not linger long when he turned and gazed up at his beloved friends again.

"I remember some words," said Wordsmith, "about the 'height of pride and the pride of height, an offense to the one who rules unseen.' Is this what was meant?"

"Your tower was tall," said Beauty. "Why was it not an offense as well?"

"I think," Wordsmith responded eventually, "that the difference is this: my tower was built from the top down, and not by human hands. Fame's has been built from the bottom up, and was built by nothing but human effort.

"And I lived in the heights by invitation, and not by my own demands."

The Child stopped in front of the ruins of Covenant's House.

"Are we not in our greatest danger here?" asked Freeblade. "We know that they seek the life of the Child and our own lives as well. We are so few, and we bear but a single sword between us and our enemies. What shall we do?"

"What we have been doing all along," shrugged Wordsmith. "Follow the Child. He alone knows where he is going and what he must do when he comes there."

"At last," Freeblade said, "the Child has come to the House of Covenant." His voice betrayed no particular emotion, and he himself was unsure which of his mixed feelings held the upper sway.

They entered the ruined building. The Child seemed at home and did not wander aimlessly among the fallen stones as the others did.

But he did lead Wordsmith and Freeblade directly to one of the deeper corners where Wordsmith's tower had once crept down from the sky. He began to dig and they with him, not knowing what he sought, but being careful that no rocks would tumble down upon their heads.

The Child scraped away a final layer of sand and revealed a wooden box.

"That is Candle's box," said Wordsmith, wiping dirt and sweat from his face with one hand.

The Child nodded, without lifting his face from his work.

"How did he know it was there?" asked Freeblade. "I myself had forgotten it."

When the Child had excavated along all four sides of the box, Freeblade leaned over the Child and delicately lifted it from the hole.

The three searchers returned to the others, joining them at rest in a corner where they could not readily be seen from the street.

"What is that?" Deedtester asked.

"It is the casket with Covenant's cloak in it," replied Freeblade heavily as he set it down on the uneven earth.

The Child began to pry at the lid, and Wordsmith helped him open it. Once the lid had been set aside, the Child lifted out the dirty, stained garment and stretched it over his knees. With his tiny but strong hands, he carefully tore the cowl from the cloak. There had been no seam there, but the cloth parted easily for the Child's fingers and left no ragged edge.

He draped the mottled cowl around his own neck under his cloak, and put the beggar's cloak back into the box.

Then he stood, handed the box to Wordsmith and motioned

them all to follow him.

"Now where?" asked Freeblade. "Is there any place more dangerous than here?"

There was, and the Child led them directly to it.

The rim of the arena welcomed them, and the Child walked straight to the half-buried edge of the Judgment Stone. Standing in its shadow, he set the casket aside and began to scrape a hole in the sand. He squared the depression a few inches deep, took the casket from Wordsmith and set it in the sand. They watched, fascinated, as it slowly sank from sight. The sand drifted itself smooth again and left no traces of the Child's work, as though a whirlpool had sunk itself in the sand.

He stood and smiled. Wordsmith wondered why all these things had happened, but no answer was given to him.

"Let us leave," urged Freeblade. "We are not safe here." He gazed at the Child, awaiting directions, but the Child gave none.

"Back to the House, then," he said. "It is the only familiar place left."

*   *   *

Under the watchful eyes of Freeblade, the Child slept that night in the crook of Beauty's arm. Wordsmith seized the advantage of the darkness and led Deedtester, Joykeeper and Seaswallower in a cautious circle of Glory, watching every action and listening to every word around them.

When they returned, they held counsel together in the cool darkness of the fallen stones.

"Have you seen Brightface or Binder?" asked Beauty immediately.

Her husband frowned and shook his head. "We have seen none from Heartshope, though many have flooded the town. Glory is awash with refugees, and they cannot easily withstand another misfortune. The fires, the walking dead, the new river from a melting mountain with the face and eyes of a magic child—all these things have ravaged their senses and worn them down. Another sign, another terror, another wonder will likely drive them to madness. Food is scarce and will grow scarcer as all the people of the land are driven into Glory.

"And there is no more death in Glory," he whispered. "No one dies, for it is said that Fame has cast a mighty spell."

"Is this true?" asked Freeblade.

Wordsmith nodded. "I have seen the delay of death with my own eyes, but there is darkness behind the truth. Men, women and children still fall ill, are wounded and suffer—but no one dies. They lie paralyzed, bloodless, broken, but still they live! The suffering does not end."

"This is worse than death," said Freeblade, "to suffer without healing and without death."

"Nor is that the only shadow behind the miracle. Where death has been abolished, birth has become a victim as well. As Candle feared when he lived in Glory, there are no babies due, nor have any been born for some time. Moonflower, it seems, is the only woman with child."

They pondered the news in silence until Wordsmith resumed. "Fame claims that his magic also melted Lonely Mountain and created the river that still grows and will one day connect us with the sea."

"We *are* connected, though he knows it not," said Deedtester.

They slept fitfully, wondering what the next day would bring.

* * *

With the dawn, Wordsmith felt the warm breath of the Child on his cheek. Once more the Child seemed to be in a hurry, and after a hasty breakfast of what was left in their packs, he led them into the crowded and frantic streets. They went to the nearest gate, and there the Child indicated that he wanted to ride on Wordsmith's shoulders. Wordsmith lifted him and waited expectantly for further direction.

The Child merely sat on his perch and looked intently at the crowds. The people there saw, and were seen by and drawn into the luminous eyes. Some passed by but were changed; others were changed and came to stand in silent wonder by the silent Child. Others broke the gaze of the Child's eyes and continued on, feeling somehow colder inside than they had been.

Each one drawn to the Child came and touched his hand, and a spark of delight passed from the one to the other and back again. The crowds moved on, and others came to the Child. Those who had come before looked back longingly yet content for now.

"Not even Covenant had this effect," whispered Beauty.

"No," murmured Wordsmith. "Freeblade, I do not think your sword is needed now, but do stand very near, with your hand on your hilt."

His caution was not misplaced, for where a whole multitude could see the Child, a soldier could see him as well.

At last one did, and brought a dozen more with him. Wordsmith and Freeblade saw them at the far edge of the crowd, pushing their way toward the Child.

Wordsmith swung the Child into his arms and began to slide away, while Freeblade quietly drew his sword. But he had no need to use it, for they were saved by the ugly mood of the crowd. The people cared not why the soldiers were there, and turned against them in anger and fear and frustration— not with weapons but with words, hurling a weight of questions and abuse against them that they could not beat back with shields. No one would dare oppose Fame to his face, but in the safety of the faceless crowd anything could happen.

The wary soldiers slowed, retreated and came again, but by the time they forced a path through the people, the Child and his bearers were gone.

* * *

All roads led to Glory, eventually, and eventually all the

refugees fled there. Nine great gates opened into Glory, and it seemed as if the Child stood at them all that day. No one entered Glory without coming, at one turning or another, face-to-face with the solemn waif, seated on Wordsmith's shoulders or standing on a fallen wall to search the faces of all those who passed.

The three from Heartshope also watched faces, hoping to see the familiar features of the Company and not soldiers' grim expressions.

* * *

"I begin to understand the Child's silence and his words," said Wordsmith that night when they huddled in the rubble of the House. "The time is past for debates and for talking and for vain postures; the only thing that may be done now is to stand with the Child or against him. There are no other choices."

He took a deep breath. "Covenant came to raise judgment and rouse wrath. I, Wordsmith, was called to hear and preserve the words of Covenant. Freeblade was called to protect the ones who came after Covenant and the Child. Beauty was summoned to run the House of Covenant, to care for Wordsmith and to give away the love she found so late in life.

"And the Child? The Child came not with more words but with open arms. The Child came to call; the warrior stands to protect those the Child has called. Do they choose him? Or does he choose them? It is all the same in the end. The Child does not need to speak or to teach or to do. He exists to love and be loved. That is his essence, his desire and his mission."

Wrapping themselves around that wisdom, they went to sleep.

* * *

Morning found them near the gates again, offering the Child's silent welcome to the crowds, both to those who entered fleeing from the country and to those who seethed in the streets looking for hope and deliverance.

SEVENTEEN

Bold
Men and
Banners

M ISERY SETTLED ON THE TOWN OF GLORY. THE FLAMES were visible on all sides, and tempers and temperatures soared.

One could barely hear above the confused roar of the crowds, assembled in any one place not to see something happen but because they had nowhere else to go.

There was no more room indoors, and neither rest nor peace anywhere. Still the desperate refugees squeezed themselves into Glory, and still the Child was there to greet them, and still the soldiers arrived too late to find him.

"Where *are* Binder and the others?" asked Wordsmith once again. "If they were within these walls, surely we would have found each other."

"I do not know," answered Beauty sadly. "Either he is waiting or something has happened to him."

"I see nothing but fire in the glass," said Freeblade. "It may be working, but it tells me nothing now."

A fresh rumble of noise rose from the gate, and the people pressed back into even tighter bunches as a magnificent parade of men, women, children and animals entered Glory.

"There they are!" shouted Freeblade. "They are the last, but not the least!"

"Wild animals!" someone screamed, and the general panic deepened, though the guard of bears and wolves and other fierce beasts made no horrid sounds and threatened no one. Within their ranks came the smaller and slower beasts bearing the remainder of the Company of Covenant, old and young and great and small alike, many with smaller animals in their arms or hands or pockets. A vast cloud of birds circled above, the tiny flying with the taloned and the swift waiting for the cumbersome.

Wordsmith pressed his way forward, and they found no hindrance from the furred guards. A cheer rose from the Company when they saw the Child, and Freeblade steered them on to the ruins of the House.

Warmed past comfort by the approaching fires, the gates were closed for a final time. There was no one left to keep out, but the gesture was made in the feeble hope of holding the flames at bay a little longer.

*   *   *

At the House the wanderers unloaded their burdens.

"And where shall we all sleep?" Binder asked. "There is little left here but rubble."

"Yes," said Lionheart. "It looks as though what is left will collapse at any moment. No wonder it has been left alone, even when lodging can scarcely be found."

Wordsmith pointed out the roofless halls and broken corridors that still might be safe for passage. "We too thought it was destroyed, and fit for nothing but the honor of an ancient and holy place. But it still shelters us and bids us welcome again."

"We have found enough room here," said Beauty, "though it is not so grand as we once had."

"This House has life," said Wordsmith, "the kind of life that cannot be created."

"Or destroyed," added Beauty.

"Though these are only the bones of the House," said Wordsmith, "still these bones have left us less than desolate in a desperate town in desperate times."

Candle dumped heavy saddlebags on the ground. "Gold is useless now," he sighed. "I can buy gold with bread and water, but not bread and water with gold. There is no place left for refuge, and no place left to hide from the flames. Either the fire stops or we die."

"The Child does not seem to think so," answered Wordsmith. "He does not appear to be concerned about either death or the flames."

*　*　*

Wordsmith with some of the Company went out quietly to see if food could be had.

While searching, Skymarker spotted one familiar face, a man who frantically waved a hammered band of gold, seeking exchange for a flask of water. There were no takers, and at last the man slammed the useless trophy to the ground and vanished into the crowd.

Skymarker recovered the battered band and smiled at the mark still graven upon it. He slipped it into his pocket, hoping he could someday return it to the grave of the man who had made his freedom possible.

Lionheart, carrying Woodswaif on his shoulders, turned a corner and came face-to-face with his mother and his sister. Neither noticed him until he spoke their names, and even then neither recognized him.

"I am Damon," he said, "or Lionheart, as I am called now."

"You can't be my son," the older woman replied coldly. "He

was taken by the lions."

Lionheart smiled. "That is more true than you know—I was indeed taken by the lions, and now I am one of their own." His smile disappeared as he turned to his sister. "I remember well the night you left your child to die on the rock," he flared.

She made a face. "That was only a girl," she said.

"As you were only a girl—once," replied Lionheart, "but my father would never have exposed *you* to die. And your daughter is well and growing, no thanks to you. Her name," he added, swinging the child down from his shoulders, "is Woodswaif. I saved her, and a beggar saved us, and a lioness nursed her."

His sister was speechless as Lionheart continued, addressing his mother. "And that night you let her take your own husband to the same rock?"

His mother moved closer to him. "I loved him," she murmured, "but I could no longer care for him." She peered more closely at his face. "And Damon was a hairless boy," she continued, "but you have a mane like a lion."

"The scars are still there," he answered. "And where is your husband?" he asked his sister. "He also had a hand in this."

"He died of fright," she said defiantly, "not long after we were set upon by lions."

"You deserved to be set upon," he said, "and it was I who set them upon you. I watched you drop my father—our father—on the rock to die, and it was I who roared and my friends who chased you away. I took him from the wilderness, and he is alive today."

She hit Lionheart with her doubled fist. He grabbed his sister's hand in his before she could strike a second time.

"Be careful," he warned. "You might hit your daughter instead." She pulled away, and he dropped her hand. "And he is not dead any longer, is he?" he continued, and saw the horror in her eyes.

"You may be my boy, after all," his mother said quietly.

"You say he is alive?" She took his hand, and his heart softened toward them.

"Come with me," he urged them both. "My father is well, and is ready to forgive you. Woodswaif still needs your love—and there are others you should meet."

He smiled down at his mother, not knowing that she saw in his face then what Lionheart had once seen in the beggar's smile.

Behind her, his sister walked away and did not turn her face back to see.

* * *

The searchers returned nearly empty-handed. "This food will have to be enough," said Wordsmith. "It may not feed us all, but let us not be miserly with it. Eat, for it may be our last meal."

They ate, and shared their meal with the animals; there seemed to be enough, for now. No one knew what would come later.

"I did not think we would return here," said Binder.

"Where else can we go?" asked Wordsmith. "Fame has not come against us here, at least so far. I wonder why he is biding his time, even in this terror he cannot control."

Two things happened at the same time.

Behind them, on the tallest jut of fallen rock, the Child climbed to his feet and raised the bloody cowl of Covenant over his head as a banner.

And in the very near distance, Fame raised his own standard above the unfinished Tower. His sign of power brought a gradual silence, and the crowds shifted in the streets to see as the news spread.

Each banner bearer could clearly see the other, for the buildings that once had lain between them had been torn down to build the Tower.

The Company turned to watch the Child, a living banner with his own banner against the backdrop of the flames and the menace of their enemies. The crowds craned their necks to the stone sky above them and waited for word from Fame.

When a full but uneasy calm had finally fallen, Fame's voice descended to them with deep authority.

"Behold the rebels!" he proclaimed, pointing at the Child and his supporters. "The makers of trouble, the people who have brought the evils of fire and flame upon you! They hide behind the cloak of a powerless child and a dead man."

"How should we answer him?" whispered Beauty.

"It is the Child's challenge," murmured Wordsmith. "Let the Child speak for us, as he always has."

The Child said nothing but stood strong.

Fame raved again, leveling charges and mixing lies with the truth.

"There is the Child's answer," said Wordsmith. "Behold his face."

The Child's face glowed all the brighter as Fame's abuse rained down. Purity answered purulence, and determination conquered defamation.

"Every person in this kingdom is *here,*" whispered Wordsmith. "Dead or living, hurt or whole, old or young, but *here.*"

And every person—dead or living, hurt or whole, old or young—gazed spellbound at the two rivals. The Child, with his bloody cowl glowing red in the light from the dancing flames. Fame, atop his private mountain of stone, hurling words down on the defenseless Child.

"The flames are their dark enchantment!" cried King Fame. "But it is an illusion only! Have I not saved you? Have any died from this fire? Dread spells may fall upon a land—but I am your King, and a magic man, and I will defeat this fire."

"Who will they believe?" asked Beauty. "A raging King or a silent Child?"

"Whoever they choose to," shrugged Wordsmith, "and they will go where they see safety. It is either Fame's Tower now or the ruins of this House."

Then the Child looked down at Wordsmith, and his gaze fired words in Wordsmith's heart and compelled him to join the Child atop the rock. There he faced the multitude and answered Fame's challenge by calling directly to the people.

"The Child calls you," he shouted, "with his silent voice, and Fame called you with lies. The flames press you hard, and you can no longer avoid the Elder God. His judgment is before you, as well as his mercy.

"You have done great evil in your life, as well as great good. Does one outweigh the other? That is not the balance by which the universe is judged. Your actions are behind you, and your future is before you. You may select your future to match your past, or you may forge a new future for the rest of time. The choice is still yours, as it ever has been. But your chance to choose will not stand open forever.

"If you come to the City, you must take the hand of the Child and follow where he leads. If you will not go to the City with us, you may have whatever is left when the City is once more made plain.

"The world cannot go on burning like this. Covenant spoke of an end to all things, and now it is at hand. You may be spared, or you will be judged with the rest. You will be judged on your obedience, and not your deeds; on your steadfast hopes, and not your wishes.

"Come to the Child, come to the Elder God, come to the works that Covenant established. Choose you must, for there is only one path in life, and only two directions on it. One is either growing closer to the Elder God or drawing further away."

Then the wellspring of his words dried up, and he was content to let the silence return. He stood with the Child, holding his tiny hand, and waited to see what would happen next.

A great silence fell, and the sun crawled its way farther across the sky, barely noticed above the glare of the flames. All could see the Child and Fame, and every heart considered the two faces set against each other. The choice forced itself upon each one in the crowd, and each one chose—some reluctantly, some with joy, but all with finality. People moved, and fought, and argued, while the Child and Fame stood like silent sentinels above them.

While the masses moved, the circling fires breached the walls and gathered the gates in their hot embrace. Then houses flamed and ashed, and even the ashes were consumed.

Clumps and lines of people surged back and forth, milling but inevitablly forming new ranks in the streets. The line joining the Tower to the House thinned and wavered and then broke entirely.

Sides had been drawn, and a battle seemed at hand. But no one knew for certain what to expect. No one moved. Everyone watched and waited and gradually fell silent.

What had been a line of question and doubt and confusion became a line of decision—a line in the sand.

Wordsmith returned to Beauty's side. She was watching the faces of many of those who had eaten at Covenant's table. Some stood with her. Many stood with Fame.

"There are so few of us," she whispered to Wordsmith.

"Compared to the ones who might have come," he answered, gesturing across the gulf forming between the sides, "we are very few indeed."

"But compared to what we were we are a multitude," Freeblade reminded them.

"Wordsmith?" asked Beauty. "There are no dead among us. They have all chosen Fame."

Wordsmith looked and saw it was true. He was about to reply when a hand gripped his shoulder; he turned to see a man and a boy whom he had last seen shifting stones in a distant valley.

"Stonesetter!" he cried. "You are here! And Featherstone with you," he added, reaching down to lift the boy up for a moment.

"Where is Sabrin?" asked Wordsmith.

Stonesetter shook his head sadly. "I last saw her climbing the ramps of the Tower," he said, scarcely taking his eyes from the Child. Featherstone trotted directly to the Child and embraced him, and was embraced in return.

The time has come, thought Wordsmith, *when to choose one love is to betray another.* He was glad that no such choice had been asked of him.

* * *

"I have numbered the brave," Halfhand said, "and there are not enough of us."

"We are two," replied Freeblade, "and we have a charge to fulfill. Numbers are not for us to consider."

"But how can we defend the Child against this army?" breathed Halfhand.

"With our swords, to start with," answered Freeblade grimly. "Every victory begins with a single stroke."

"Dreadnought!" called Wordsmith.

"Yes?" answered Freeblade boldly.

"Your name is also your command," he said. "Dread nought, Freeblade!"

The warrior lifted his head higher. "It is a good name," he answered, his voice ringing with renewed power, "and I shall bear it proudly!"

The flames waited silently to see what would happen. All the universe narrowed down to this—two buildings in a place of flame and rock.

"Seize them!" Fame called from his Tower. "Feed them to the flames, and break their cursed spell!"

Freeblade's voice rang out just as clearly, though he spoke from the leveled rocks. "Oppose the Child at your peril!"

Freeblade laid a deadly web of steel before him, feeling the comfort of Halfhand fighting at his back.

The soldiers and the desperate came at them, finding little room to fight in the narrow streets. Freeblade fought until the number of his wounds increased to an agony, and still he fought on; he fought until no more blood ran in his veins, and then he fought on.

I cannot die, he exulted, *and I cannot be defeated. Can any warrior ask for more?* The sword danced in his hand, and if his heart ceased to beat he knew it not. The image of the Child drove him on, anchored his feet in the shifting sandy clay and stood him steadfast in the way.

The attackers fell back, dragging the fallen with them. In the temporary lull, Freeblade drove his sword into the ground with the last of his strength. "No more!" he cried out. The ground cracked before him. "Let no man cross this gulf again!" The crack widened and filled with a smoking churn of water from somewhere beneath the earth. The spray dashed to the edge of the sword and halted there in a sudden backswirl.

The crack circled the House, yawning wider and deeper and filling with foaming water, stranding the Company dry and isolated in the ruins.

Their enemies retreated frantically, somehow forcing space for themselves within the walls of the Tower or clinging to the ledges and crevices of its high spirals.

The streets, abandoned, were soon awash in smoking water.

Freeblade crumpled victorious to the ground, driven to what should have been death, but never defeated.

Utterly spent, the entire Company waited for the next unimaginable thing to happen.

They were not disappointed.

EIGHTEEN

Stones
and
Surprises

A SUDDEN SHIMMER OF LIGHT DREW THEIR EYES TO THE wall over the Judgment Stone. As they watched, pieces of mortar began to crack away and dust began to rise. A section of the wall over the Judgment Stone collapsed.

The surface of the Tower rippled and shuddered, the structure swayed, and a hail of smaller stones pattered down, but the Tower stood.

The Judgment Stone lifted itself from its bed in the sand and began to rise in the air. No mortal could lift it, and no mortal did. The punishment of gravity was undone, and from the darkness beneath the rock came Covenant.

Cheers quickly rose from the confusion of the Company. Fame howled from his Tower, and the sound chilled those who stood with him. The Company barely heard him, as their eyes and hearts fastened upon their beloved beggar.

"He *is* alive!" shouted Wordsmith.

Beauty clutched her husband's arm fiercely. "They *couldn't* kill someone like him!"

Covenant raised his hands, and absolute silence fell on all sides. His cloak, no longer patched or stained or bloodied, gleamed with a radiance that dazzled even the flames and beat them back dulled and disordered, dying down but not defeated, ready and patient to do the beggar's bidding.

The watchers knew, at last, who had summoned the flames.

"He is the same Covenant as ever," Beauty murmured, "yet not the same."

Covenant came to the Company, striding across the roiling water and the awful gulf beneath. He touched the dry land again, and the Company rushed to meet him. Their joy knew no bounds, and they surrounded him, Fame and enemies forgotten—afraid to touch him yet longing with all their hearts to feel his solid arms about them again.

He opened wide his arms and greeted them each by name. They accepted his love gladly—joining together in happy chaos, pressing in but not crowding, waiting for his attention yet content to wait, taking his blessing and giving it back to him even as it was given.

Then Covenant looked up to the Child standing on the ruined ramparts; upon seeing Covenant's face, the Company moved out of his path. The white-clad beggar ascended the rubble in a joy that ran far deeper than mere excitement. They approached one another slowly, with confidence and even unconscious ceremony, like old friends who had been too long apart and had joined together again at a great moment.

All the hopes the Company had ever held were summed and multiplied until they overflowed, for not only had Covenant returned but the Child was still with them.

They gathered around the rocks in the wake of the beggar's passage. Even Freeblade, worn beyond death but revived by the sight of his charge and his champion together, came near, turning his back to the strip of sandy dirt he had just defended.

Now it was a gap that would keep itself, he knew, for Covenant alone had crossed it and none had power to follow. Climbing upon the tilted rocks, he laid his bloody sword at Covenant's feet.

Halfhand, following in his leader's shadow, did the same.

It seemed a ripe time for offerings, and the others began to bring him what they had. Food, a few scraps of fine clothing, a piece of costly jewelry—Covenant needed none of these things but accepted them all with high praise and dignity.

Skymarker and Trueteller came side-by-side to deliver him the gold band already graven with his mark. The Child accepted it for Covenant, and placed it on the beggar's finger as a trophy for all to behold.

Candle came last, bulging bags in his hands. "I would gladly lay all this gold at your feet," he said, "if it were not such a useless treasure. Still, it is all I have."

Covenant smiled. "I accept it anyway, for the worth I know it has. Leave it there on the ground, and I will show you its value myself."

He is more king than beggar, thought Wordsmith, *but I will never fail to remember him as the ragged wanderer we all tried to despise and dismiss. Who could have guessed?*

Vaguely, as though at a long distance, the Company could hear Fame shouting. Though he was near, his words seemed far, and scarcely mattered to them in the glow that came from the gloried pair standing above them.

"What is he saying?" asked Wordsmith.

"It does not matter," replied Covenant, "for all his words are lies. Before this moment, his words stung and wounded and laid waste those who listened, but now you hear the true weight of all his words."

Around them in Glory wooden roofs burst into flame from

the heat and houses crumbled as their wooden beams smoldered and bent. The air was exceedingly hot, and each breath became dryer and more painful than the last. There seemed to be nothing left but fire and water and rock.

"What did Fame build his tower on?" Covenant asked in the silence.

"The Judgment Stone," answered Wordsmith.

Covenant shook his head. "Yes, the Judgment Stone, the Stone That Fell, which became the Rock of Death and now has become the Rock That Was Rolled Away. But under that, and beside that, and all around?"

"Sand," said Wordsmith, understanding at last. "Nothing but sand."

Covenant nodded. "Sand has betrayed more than one dream," he said. "Watch."

He laid hold of the Child's hand and turned to the Tower again. "Fame," he thundered, "take the rotting risen, and the dying who have abandoned life, and build your empire of the dead. In darkness and stillness is your kingdom, and your crown will never satisfy you in its nothingness."

Then Covenant spoke an awful name upon their enemies, and the hearers knew that the horrid truth had been uttered for all time. There was no longer room for denial.

Covenant and the Child turned their backs on the Tower; there was no joy on their countenances. A great shadow fell upon Fame's creation, even in the teeth of the great fires all around. The flames turned darker, tinged with a new blast of judgment.

Beauty sensed what was coming, and shuddered. She wondered if the sight of Covenant's back would be a lesser weight than the sight of his sad-angry face.

Horrified, but unable to look away, Wordsmith saw the surging waters undermine the wall, sluicing away the sand and leaving frail dark hollows behind. The Tower quivered again and began to crumble.

The flames leaped up the sheer walls of the Tower, rising with bright fingers along the stones like a waterfall flowing backwards to its source, searing and melting wherever it touched. The very rock turned to liquid fire and betrayed those who clung to it. Their screaming rose to the brassy sky, to be silenced only by the return of death.

The defiant Fame stood on his spire alone and was the last to succumb to the ravenous flames. His clothes burned first, and then his skin began to wrinkle and melt, and under his once-handsome face the watchers had a brief glimpse of the truth beneath the disguise. They were horrified for an instant, and then the flames delivered them from the sight.

The entire Tower collapsed into the water. The fires continued to burn in the midst of the depths, a bright and savage glow under the liquid sheen. The water could not quench it, but when the very rock had been consumed the sunken fires went out.

There were no traces of the Tower, no signs of anyone who had clung to it in their final moments of despair. The waters roiled and steamed below, reflecting the gleams of the flames that still burned on the rim of Glory.

The Company watched wordlessly. *How horrible*, shuddered Wordsmith, *to burn and drown at the same time*. And suddenly the smell of evil was gone from the earth. None had known what it was when it had been there, but now in its absence they knew what it had been.

Covenant turned again and gestured, and the ground rose obediently from the waters, and they saw the Judgment Stone made whole once more and rooted fast in the rock of the earth.

"It was indeed a cornerstone," Covenant said, "but not for his tower."

"What happened to the rebels?" breathed Beauty to Wordsmith.

"I don't know," answered Wordsmith. "They are not here.

Whatever came upon them, I feel it was both horribly merciful and better than they deserved."

Covenant turned to them. "It is not merely death," he said, "it is the utter absence of life, and destruction for all time. The Child has rescued all who would be rescued; there was no cure for the rest. This is the ultimate exposure, the unending horror, the terror that never ends *for them*. To us, they have already come to an end and are no more. Even their memory will fade from your minds."

"Where are they? Are they all together now?" asked Freeblade.

"If there is a place where I cannot tread," said Covenant, "a country where I cannot rule, they are there. In death and destruction they have been united, but they are separated now, and joined together only in their loneliness and desolation. In life they wished to be left alone; in death their wish shall be granted.

"But all that is a memory," he continued, and the renewed brightness in his voice lifted their hearts. "A memory, a ghost of things past, an echo of that which has served its purpose. Death is already done now and undone forever—let Time begin anew!" His words were true, for within a moment even the memory of the smell of the smoke of evil was gone, as death was swallowed up by life welling from the very heart of the earth.

Wordsmith eyed the leaping fires. "I am not afraid of the flames now," he said. "They are *his*."

NINETEEN

The Cleansing Flames

T ASTE THESE TEARS," COVENANT SAID. "THEY ARE THE LAST dewdrops of pain that anyone here shall ever shed again."

And they all wept, and considered their grief, and Covenant wept beside them. Then Covenant's eyes dried, and within a few moments a quiet but immense joy bubbled up in all their hearts and warmed its way up to their mouths and left smiles of relief and contentment there.

"And now I complete your joy," continued Covenant. "Behold!"

The ground trembled beneath them, and from the center of the ruins that had once been Covenant's House a new wonder began to rise from the depths of the earth.

And there stood the building they themselves had helped build—but now it was vaster, no longer a building but the

City, high and grand and almost too bright to see.

It was so new and amazing that they could hardly believe it—but so real and powerful they could not help but believe it. What they had formerly called reality was a dim and wavering smoke against the solidity of what now held their eyes.

The City was immaculate, but not as though it had just been fashioned; it had the look of something quite ancient that could never be weathered or damaged or stained—a holy place put aside until there were ones found worthy to enter its gates.

Even Wordsmith could find no words fit for the City; even the most splendid words he knew fell far short of holding even a glimmer of its true glory.

"Oh, Covenant!" exclaimed Beauty. "Is this now as it was then?"

"Yes," said Covenant, "save for one thing: there is no voice calling you away into the wilderness.

"The earth is yours again," he continued, "to explore and enjoy. It is one of my gifts to you."

With his words the circling flames burned away, leaping from the earth into the heavens before spiraling down into the unseen center of the City.

They looked to see what had happened to the land, expecting to see forests laid waste and the very earth scorched and smoking and lifeless.

What they saw stunned them almost as much as the sight of the City. It was still a green land, though *still* was not adequate to describe a land reborn and bursting forth with life.

The fire had both destroyed the land and renewed it. Where there had been trees, now there were forests. Where there had been deserts, now there were lush open meadows. They stared with widened eyes at vast stands of trees that had never known ruthless slashings; broad meadows where none had ever trampled a path; pure sky undimmed by the smokes and fires of those struggling to stay warm or keep away the darkness.

Where there had been death, now there was life. Where there had been life, now there was life abundant. Where Glory had been built, there was now only soft loam beneath their feet.

"My fires burned away only what was twisted and fallen," said Covenant. "All that once was good and unspoiled is now even better."

Not far away, on a broad and placid sparkling river, a renewed *Childsbreath* bobbed at anchor.

At their feet, where Candle had dumped his worthless gold, a shining path lay ready to lead their feet into the City.

"What value is gold now?" asked Covenant. "No more than any other wonder that has been wrought. Let it dazzle and delight and be here forever untarnished for all to see—no longer locked away, hoarded in that world where delight was consumed by desire."

The animals looked to him for a word, and he gave them their desire. "Go," he said simply, "the earth is good for you again."

A stream of fur and feathers and scales flowed away from them into the fresh wilderness, wrapped in the sounds of woofs and barks and howls of pleasure, high keening calls and sweet buoyant songs.

Covenant laid his hands gently on Kingsburro's flank and Roadreeler's nose. "Stay with us, if you will, for a while," he asked softly.

They stayed, dropping their faces to the ground to sample the fresh and interesting grasses that had sprouted around their hooves.

"But let us see the City first!" Covenant said to his Company. They received his words not as a command but as an invitation.

"The City holds life, and new life as well. Moonflower shall be delivered in the City, and all will celebrate the children she bears."

And then the glow around Covenant and the Child was overshadowed by an even brighter light that bloomed from the center of the City—a light so bright that all fell to their knees save Covenant and the Child. And then that same dazzle sparked from the two, and where the three lights met they merged into one light, resonating and pulsing and multiplying as high as they could see.

Then a new fire bloomed before them on the path, distorting the gold with its shimmer but melting nothing.

"This is the final fire," said Covenant. "It will not destroy *you*. It will hurt you, because it must change you, but it cannot kill you. You are beyond that now. This is a *voluntary* fire, and will bring fierce pain, but only for a few instants. Only a part of you will burn."

Still they hesitated, until the Child took Wordsmith's hand in his and walked with him into the flames. Beauty came after, and then all chose the fire.

When they stepped into the flames their cries began—but the pain of the burning was itself instantly consumed by the joy of release from their unrecognized chains.

The darkness of the vanished world no longer weighed upon them; they felt only the burdens of their own failures and weakness, and grieved for the load that had bent them low to the ground and rendered them so long blind and powerless.

The flames soared, and they felt themselves untwisted by invisible hands, with unimaginable power and unexpected tenderness. Old fears were swallowed by conquering delight, and even the old pleasures were reborn in new fashions. Broken bones forced themselves right, and old agonies evaporated.

Their hearts burst into flame within them, and they began to forget much of the pain that had enmeshed itself in their lives; the power to remember was not taken from them, but as joy replaced dread the darker memories paled and did not seem worth the effort of recall.

The flames died abruptly and left them standing on the golden path.

Wordsmith looked at Covenant and thanked him. "It is not a choice one would make over again, but it has its blessings for having been endured."

The light from the City, while not dimming at all, gradually became less painful to their eyes.

"Wordsmith," cried Beauty, "what is happening? Is the light going away?"

"No," he replied, smiling.

"But I can look at it now," she continued.

"The fire has not changed—but we have," he answered, looking to Covenant and receiving his nod of confirmation. "The firebath has made all of us new and whole. *This* is what eyes were first created to see!"

And as they stepped forward into the new light, their shadows shriveled into nothingness like the pain of their past. The first rays pierced them, with a sudden shock of power, but the beams encouraged their hearts and drew them closer. They smelled a sacred smell—a new smell that woke memories too old and deep to be merely their own.

Wrapped in light and the pure scent, they faced Covenant and the Child.

TWENTY

Crowns and Kings

"COME!" CALLED COVENANT, AND THE SMILE OF THE CHILD echoed him. "There is a crown to be given, and after that he who is crowned shall give crowns to the faithful. The City has been brought forth again, and the Child shall be its King!"

"Look!" called Beauty. "In the gates!"

There beneath an arch another crowd waited—a crowd led by some Wordsmith recognized, including the unbent and perfected figure of Woebearer.

"Who are they?" asked Brightface.

"They are the ones who came before you," smiled Covenant. "They tasted death before you, and so tasted life first as well. The City has been their home," he continued, "but it could not yet be their kingdom. Come!" he beckoned them all forward.

The faithful of all the ages streamed through the gate and joined the Company. Wordsmith looked, and pondered, and understood why some of the graves had emptied after Covenant's death, and why as well none of the newly risen dead had joined the Company in the last stand against Fame. Covenant's chosen dead were already before him, and had already been rewarded with the City.

Kingsburro drifted forward and gently nudged the Child. Roadreeler, on the other side, nibbled deftly at the edge of Covenant's sleeve.

Covenant turned first to Kingsburro. "And now, patient one, beast of burden to many, come and bear a final burden that is no burden at all."

The Child mounted Kingsburro and led Roadreeler along the golden path into the City, and vanished from sight.

"He goes to bring forth the treasures of the City," proclaimed Covenant, and his words fell like a wondrous trumpet blast on their ears.

Kingsburro is honored, thought Lionheart.

Covenant turned to him and answered his unspoken question. "He is worthy of honor, for he is patient, he loves all who love him, and he does whatever is asked of him. Can you say as much in praise of many people?"

"No," said Lionheart. "It is fit that he should show us the way."

Then the Child returned, with two large ornate chests balanced over Roadreeler's back. The Child rode Kingsburro and carried a single small chest in his hands.

Covenant helped the Child unload the animals, and then he turned them loose into their green reward with a caress and a murmur of praises.

Then Covenant opened the smaller chest and lifted a golden crown from the silken folds within.

He bent to place it on the head of the beaming Child.

"Behold the King!" he announced.

And then Covenant raised the Child to the highest throne of all: his own shoulders.

"Behold the King!" echoed Wordsmith as the beggar crowned himself. The Company applauded and knelt and rejoiced all at the same time.

"Who crowns, and who is crowned?" murmured Beauty through her tears.

"Covenant crowns the Child, but then the Child is Covenant's crown," said Freeblade.

"I did not know it was possible to share a crown," Candle said.

"We all know now," answered Halfhand. "Two can indeed wear a single crown."

Then Covenant lowered the Child and turned to his waiting friends.

He called Wordsmith's old name first, and then the new name he had given him, and then he beckoned him forward to receive a jeweled wooden box from one of the great chests before him.

When Wordsmith opened the box, he found a dazzling diamond there with a new name graven on it, a name that only Covenant knew and only Wordsmith could read—a new name that brought him unutterable delight and a complete sense of contentment and fulfillment—a name that was meant for him and he for it. The diamond was fixed in a broad gold band, woven with airy strength. The Child drew it forth and revealed it as a crown. He handed it to Covenant, who gently placed it upon Wordsmith's head.

Beauty cheered him, and the others joined her in response to the value of the man revealed. For the first time in his life, Wordsmith knew the taste of rightful praise and the honor that did not corrupt and could not be corrupted.

Beauty was called next, and the Child drew forth a like box and a like crown for Covenant's hands to fit to her head.

One by one the beggar king called the faithful, and still the chests yielded boxes to yield their treasures and rewards. All were glorified, and those who beheld the different glories could not say which was the greater, nor did the thought occur to them. The time for comparisons had come and gone.

When they had all received crowns, Wordsmith began to sing. The rest listened enchanted to the words, and joined him the second time in praise to the Child, Covenant and the Elder God.

At the peak of his singing Wordsmith took a few steps forward, hesitant, surprised to find no pain there at long last.

Then he began to dance.

His exuberance was contagious, and soon the others danced with him and behind him, surprised by the depths of their own wells of irrepressible peace.

Covenant lifted the Child to his shoulders again. They smiled together, and the air sweetened about them.

With Wordsmith leading them in song, the joyful multitude followed the twin kings deeper into the City toward the light.

—AFTERWORD—

Myth and legend lie to the north, prophecy to the south, and parable and allegory to the east and west. But what are these stories, if none of the above? The three books that make up Tales of the Forgotten God do not fit comfortably into any category save one—the kind of books I most enjoy reading.

There: the secret's out. I wrote these books for an audience of one. I have been pleased and surprised, since then, to discover a few people eager to read over my shoulder.

Where have these books come from? They appear to bloom full grown on the store shelves, like an overnight *ex nihilo* event, but appearances are deceptive. Like all things born of human agents, there was hope and uncertainty in their planning and pain and wonder in their birth and maturation. The beggar first came walking through my imagination in the middle 1970s. I wasn't at all sure who he was or what his business might be.

The background against which he was operating seemed clear enough. The landscape was an undeveloped country in a limited political and geographical landscape—bounded by hills and mountains beyond which people had never gone. It had unnumbered small villages, and only one great town in the center. The town was the finest place in all the land, but some people had heard rumors of a City that far surpassed it. The problem was that no one knew exactly how to return to the City.

The beggar moved in a world where other gods were recognized and the Elder God only dimly remembered by the masses. In the miracles he performed and the challenges he set forth he was like a prophet, making the way straight and plain for a larger and later act by another. But he was also obviously a Christ-figure, though just as obviously not Jesus in disguise. He had a different kind of ministry in mind and at hand. He was very low profile and individual-oriented and seemed to specialize in inverting people's perceptions and restoring them to their proper positions. His agenda was never quite what one would guess. He did many things that the prophets did, but he did a few things that even the prophets didn't do. He seemed to be a cross between a prophet and a preincarnation appearance of Christ. (We don't get to see very much of Jesus as Melchizedek or "the angel of the Lord" in the Bible, but the hints are there.) He didn't behave exactly like anyone I had run across in either literature or the Scriptures.

Whoever he was, his compelling actions called to be set down on paper. So I recorded his first adventure, and then another, and then three more over the next ten years.

Those five stories became part of a collection that eventually drew the interest of Cindy Bunch-Hotaling and Andy Le Peau at InterVarsity Press. They asked if the tales concerning the beggar could be expanded into a novel. With some hesitation, I said yes. They promptly informed me they thought it would make a great trilogy.

So be it.

The beggar was only waiting for such an opportunity to return. The original five stories became six foundational tales for *The Beggar King*—"The Dead of Night," "A Night for Names," "After the Rain," "Trial by Fire," "Before Winter" and "Beauty and the Feast." More tales blossomed from the tail of what I had once thought was the last; the fruit of the next two years' labor is contained in these pages.

The beggar revealed his name—Covenant—and remained consistent with what he had first made plain about himself. His character grew, and his works continued and began to add up to a comprehensive whole that could be sensed only by those who accepted his viewpoint. I did not see where the set of stories would come to a close. As in life, the end was not clearly in sight when I stood at the beginning. What happened in the second and third books was as much a surprise to me as to anyone; what did occur was more than I had expected and has satisfied me immensely—and should serve as a reminder that behind every Wordsmith telling a story there is One who first brings the images to life.

And, as with any authentic work, these books are a confession of my hopes and convictions as well as a revelation of my influences.

Scripture can roughly be divided into *information, commands* and *promises;* the images here are born from my continued thirst for promises that are still everlastingly true even when my mind can absorb no more facts and my obedience has been found lacking. In the end, it is not what I (or anyone else) have done but what God has done that will make the eternal differences in the history of the universe; it is our privilege to be allowed to choose sides before the final stand and the final judgment come to pass.

Power. Power flows here, and perhaps no place more obviously than in the naming and renaming of names.

To name a thing is to have power over it. God gave Adam his name, and God could also have named the animals in the Garden, but he didn't; they reported directly to Adam, and it was up to the man to name them. "And whatever he named them, that was their name."

This permission that was power continued in Adam's descendants as a pattern, but it was not absolute, for God overrode human-given names on more than one occasion. Abram was rechristened Abraham; John the Baptist was headed for life as Zechariah until his father of the heaven-sealed lips set the record straight; and Simon the easily swayed found a new identity as Peter the immovable rock.

Genesis 35:10 is typical of Covenant's approach to names and the blessings of names. "And God said to him, 'Your name is Jacob; no longer shall your name be called Jacob, but Israel shall be your name.' So his name was called Israel" (NASB).

The name was always changed for a reason—and the old and new names usually meant something in the native tongue. "And its name was called . . . , which means . . ." is a common Old Testament refrain and formula. (Note the phrase "And they called his name . . . ," as though the name itself were separate and secret and they were just labeling it something else as a temporary convenience, leaving the deeper name unvoiced and unchanged.)

Nor are the final chapters of this book an accidental refrain, for one of the final promises given us in Revelation is the prospect of a new name, a secret name, a true name fit for both the speaker and the hearer.

Choices. These tales portray life the way I wish it were: simpler (though not necessarily easier) and yet more magical at the same time. But the choices are the same as those we make, and the choices are real and make a difference in every moment of our lives.

The choices of God are made plain as well. He is the unseen (that is, unwatched for) manipulator behind every event. He cannot be avoided, he cannot be hurried, and he cannot be thwarted. All things—strange or sad, incredible or tragic—are taken up and woven together by the only One who knows what the patterned threads look like from on high. The trilogy is not a deliberate attempt to disguise gospel as fantasy, but to imagine in words what God might have done with another land in another time—and perhaps in a different universe altogether. His purpose would have been the same, his methods similar, and the results identical. But all the tiny details would be vastly and wonderfully different, for God never needs to do anything the same way twice.

Some influences upon me will be plain, even though I didn't deliberately copy anyone or try to create a book that leaned too heavily upon another's work. Yet how can a voracious reader turned writer not be saturated with echoes of his favorite authors?

C. S. Lewis and George MacDonald—they of the baptized imaginations—are my acknowledged masters. And there is G. K. Chesterton, the prince of paradox, who was so adept at creating tilted madmen and leaning idiots who turned out to be the only ones with a real grasp of the truth.

The recurring images of (and emphasis on) the City are largely derived from Augustine, mostly via Charles Williams.

Some sparks and images come from the written and recorded works of Ray Bradbury, Loren Eiseley, Eric Clapton, Jackson Browne, Dogwood and others.

Other influences are not so obvious. For example, "Trial Without Fire" *(The Beggar King)* was sparked in part by a winter's overnight writing session as I lay parked on our foldout couch with a sleeping child against each elbow. A pair of the household cats (including the *big* one) joined the pileup; the result was surprisingly warm—both physically and emotionally. That cozy assembly helped keep at bay both the external frost and the three-in-the-morning loneliness that tends to haunt writers at work (whether they're actually working or not).

These books have been dedicated to my family, and references to them are scattered throughout. I wish them special joy in future years as they recognize the familiar shifted into a new and equally wondrous setting.

Lastly, this writing has also been therapy. Many who read this trilogy will assume that the words were written with polished ease out of the excess delight of my heart—but the truth is far different. Every passage was squeezed out of me in fragments, more often than not against the suffocating pressure of severe depression, beneath the blanket of dark melancholia. And so it is true in yet another sense that I wrote these words not for you but for me. What was given to me in the abundant grace of Christ was a gift for difficult times—and what I have been given I will gladly share.

Words can heal as they are heard in the head and travel down to the heart; a further round of healing takes place when the words are placed on paper and seen to be worthy and true. The next round of healing is to hear that these stories have comforted others as well—for the only possible and lasting comfort offered to us comes in the form of the Story which begins in Genesis and does not end (thank God!) with Revelation.

In him,
Dan Hamilton
Indianapolis, Indiana
August 1994